JEET

Jeet Thayil was born _____ into a Syrian Christian family in Kerala, and educated at Jesuit schools in Bombay, Hong Kong and New York.

Kerala's Syrian Christians trace their church to St. Thomas, who arrived on the Malabar coast around 50 AD and converted thirteen Hindu families to Christianity, or so tradition has it. Jeet's grandmother, Chachiamma Jacob, was the last of the family who recited from memory the hour-long service in Aramaic, Malayalam and Sanskrit that still defines the faith.

ALSO BY JEET THAYIL

Fiction
*Low*
*The Book of Chocolate Saints*
*Narcopolis*

Poetry
*Collected Poems*
*These Errors are Correct*
*English*
*Apocalypso*
*Gemini* (Two-Poet Volume with Vijay Nambisan)

As Editor
*The Penguin Book of Modern Indian Poets*
*The Bloodaxe Book of Contemporary Indian Poets*
*Divided Time: India and the End of Diaspora*

Libretti
*Babur in London*
*Talk is Cheap*

JEET THAYIL

# Names of the Women

VINTAGE

1 3 5 7 9 10 8 6 4 2

Vintage is part of the Penguin Random House group of companies whose
addresses can be found at global.penguinrandomhouse.com

Copyright © Jeet Thayil 2021

Jeet Thayil has asserted his right to be identified as the author of this
Work in accordance with the Copyright, Designs and Patents Act 1988

First published in Vintage in 2022
First published in hardback by Jonathan Cape in 2021

penguin.co.uk/vintage

A CIP catalogue record for this book is
available from the British Library

ISBN 9781529113822

Printed and bound in Great Britain by Clays Ltd, Elcograf S.p.A.

The authorised representative in the EEA is Penguin Random House
Ireland, Morrison Chambers, 32 Nassau Street, Dublin D02 YH68

Penguin Random House is committed to a sustainable future
for our business, our readers and our planet. This book is made
from Forest Stewardship Council® certified paper.

*To Chachiamma Jacob,*
*Ammu George,*
*Sheba Thayil,*
*Tia Anasuya*
*& Mindy Kaur Gill*

# 1

Mary, write that they nailed the left wrist first. I heard the sound I made as I broke, my blood and beloved bones leaving me at last. I was tied to the beam so long the feeling in my hands had died, odd mercy when they hammered in the nail. I no longer knew wrist or hand or arm. I knew only pain, as vast and old as the sky. I no longer cared about the body I had borrowed and loved. Its time had passed, as all things pass. I was conscious only of the breaking. They placed one foot over the other and I felt in my calves the strangeness of the posture. I felt the twist of pleasure. I heard myself. I was inside the sound of my splintering. Write, Mary, that everything follows from that moment, the death, the return, the centuries of turmoil and ecstasy, at the moment I fell into the dream and the dream became real. I remembered that when I was a child of seven we went to a town nearby and on the way back we stopped at an inn. I saw a family eating their evening meal. I saw the look on the face of the woman as she put a morsel into her mouth and chewed, and the words came to me unbidden. Take me, Abba, I wish only to die. I saw her face and I knew what would follow as surely as mourning follows the feast and tears follow laughter. Aloud I cried, Abba, I wish to die. And here he has granted my wish, my dear father. More than any of the good and terrible things that happened to me, I remember the day the black wish came, how suddenly, how heavily and for always, twenty-six years ago when I saw a woman eat a meal, and I saw the days wear away one by one, and I shunned the house of feasting for the house of tears. Because that day it pleased my father to show me the face of suffering, and it was his face I saw, the beauty of it and the terribleness that no language can describe. They say it requires no great courage of heart or any great will to look upon such beauty, yet how partial is their understanding. My enemies have not seen the light of his brow, the terrible light that renders them insensible. Then how can they speak of courage or beauty? For it was the face of our Lord I saw upon the woman and it filled me with the sadness. I watched her eat her meal and I recognised the desolation that had come upon her. I knew the fate of the flesh, the fate we eat and take inside us all the holy day, and I wished only to die. All things come alike to all. That day or the next day or a day soon after, my mother told me of the angel who had come to her whose name she had forgotten, everything forgotten but the particularity of his raiment and his words. Imma, I said to her, Gabriel was his name, don't you remember? She said, I remember only what he said, that my son would die on the cross, the terrible words that made me forget every other thing. Then she told me to live the days of my life fully. To learn the ways of men. To seek in my spirit first, then in my mind and at last in my body. To give myself to the answer. To give myself unto wine or pleasure if that was what I wished. But to hurry, for time counts his coin and will settle his account one way or the other. This is what my mother said the angel said, and I say it to you, Mary. I learned the ways of men for they were easy to learn. I learned to disdain the moaning bed, the want and begetting followed by the usual oblivion, the wine and feasting followed by the usual remorse. I learned more in the desert than ever I learned in the houses of men. And I say unto you who hear these words two hundred or two thousand years after me, what good are the victuals if you cannot eat them, but a stranger takes and eats and is satisfied? This is the way of vanity and darkness. You may be the master of a hundred houses and yet your name will be darkness. For how can you feast when your brother fasts? How can you laugh when your brother's house is in mourning and your mother tears herself from broken-heartedness? How can you love when your brother, your child, hangs above you, splintered across?

# 2

She wakes too early. She has forgotten how to sleep in the same way she had forgotten how to laugh. Those things she once accepted without question are far from her now. They are part of someone else's life, someone accustomed to the comforts of home and an unchanging place in the world. Now she sleeps in snatches and wakes mystified, as if something terrible has happened while her eyes were shut. If only she had been alert all would be changed, he would be alive, the days on the hill a twist of the mind, nothing more.

In the early dark she goes out to the courtyard to wash. The house comes fully awake. A lamp is lit. She hears the scrape of a bucket lowered into the well. She is wrapping a shawl around her shoulders when Rebekah limps in from the servants' quarters with a jug of water. But she cannot drink or eat. She cannot think. She can only say the words that have been repeating in her head through the wakeful hours of the night, as if she were trying to cast a spell and spell out a protection against death. But protection for whom, for herself or the one who died? When everything has been severed, what will remain? A memory, the touch of a hand, someone saying her name. Barely moving, her lips repeat the two whispered syllables that make up her vigil and prayer: *Not dead*.

She must hurry to the tomb the one called Joseph of Arimathaea made for himself, even if tomb is too grand a word for a hole hacked into the rock, and in that hole a shelf, the dead air washed with a muddy light that rises up from the ground, smelling of insects and dust, a smell that stays in your head for days. Not suitable in any way as a burial place for the Rabbuni. How did it come to pass, such a man laid to rest in so rough a cave, a hole borrowed from a passing stranger? And isn't it true that he might have wanted it this way, who spurned all finery and ease?

She is ready to leave, but Rebekah brings her a bowl and she stares at it unseeing, troubled by a memory from her childhood. The old woman has been with her family for as long as she can remember. She was a second mother to her, because her mother was so far gone into her own troubles she could not care for her daughter. When she was nine years old her father secured the services of a priest to instruct her older brother in the stories of the scripture. But her brother had shown no aptitude for study, had taken after his mother, was subject to fears and terrors that had no roots in reality. The priest came each afternoon and recited prayers that her brother would try to memorise. One afternoon she hid in the alcove near the prayer room and repeated silently each of the priest's lessons while her brother, distracted by the light, blurted the man's words at random, words such as 'mercy' and 'terror' and phrases such as 'smite mine enemies' and 'flatten the godless in their filth'. When the priest intoned a lesson about 'the

5

great whore's pendulous dugs and disease-ridden sex' she found she could not repeat it. But her brother, suddenly alert, shouted, 'Disease sex, disease sex.' And that was when she saw her mother by her side, holding a blue bowl of fruit, her eyes shiny pools of oil that filled and ebbed, filled and overflowed. Go, she whispered. You are a girl child, don't you know? It is your wickedness to grasp for the fruits vouchsafed to men. As she hissed at her stricken daughter she shielded the blue bowl with her hand. Shielded it from whom? Then it struck her. It's me, the fruit is for my brother and she thinks I might snatch it. The next day her mother made Rebekah scrub her with a birch branch. She watched over the washing, saying the servant must scrub harder, scrub until her daughter's skin was raw and ridged with welts. Once a week that year the scrubbing continued. Even now she approaches a bath with reluctance, her skin puckering at the sight of a pail of water in a windowless room.

In the lamplight the grains on the wood are clear as grit in unleavened bread. Something glistens in the bowl like cut snails or worms, or innards draped with translucent slime. 'Grapes,' Rebekah says, still holding the bowl, 'and pears from the orchard, with some of the new honey I brought from the market.' She takes only a cup of fresh water, which displeases her old servant. The old woman holds her tongue, though she cannot stop herself from making the usual rebuke: 'You spend more time out of the house than the master used to. This is not the way of good women.'

'Better to be alive than good,' she says. 'What happens to the good men and women of this world? They are the first to die and we are afraid even to mourn.'

'Hush,' says Rebekah, covering her ears. 'No.'

'It's true, they die first, in agony.'

'Hush,' Rebekah says, her voice tight with fear.

She takes nothing with her but the spiced oil she has asked Rebekah to prepare, to preserve the body. Now the words return that resounded all night: *Not dead*. And she remembers a time before the Rabbuni, when there was more than one voice in her head and they all said the same thing, *Why not die?* Her bad days, when she worried that insanity was a family curse, days that are behind her now because of the Rabbuni. Is he dead? And if he is dead, what of the God that allows such a man to die, whose innocence was written on his face? What of the God who murders infants in their sleep? Who massacres the guiltless and condemns them to torture? The God who raises the guilty and rewards them with land and titles? What of the God's unquenchable taste for blood? Would the Rabbuni's death endow the God with a change of heart so he would choose mercy over vengeance? If not, his crucifixion and death were as meaningless as the deaths of the innocents who preceded him. But it could not be so. The death of his Son would change the God from the God of terror to the God of love, would it not?

At no time during the events of the recent past did it seem possible to her that he would die, not when he was arrested, not during the march to Golgotha or the halting climb to the crest of the hill, not when he was nailed to the beams and the cross raised against the darkening sky. It hadn't seemed possible then and it doesn't seem possible now. Even if the world had changed entirely in one night, how could it be that he was no longer of it, who promised that a new world was possible and nothing would harm him or those who followed him? They were safe, he said, protected from the future that lumbered towards them borne on giant wings. They felt its heat. They heard the speed at which it approached. And still they believed. They should have known they were on the verge of a cataclysm. Then they might have been better prepared for the time that was upon them, the time of desolation, when a Levantine, or a Canaanite, or any stranger faced extermination because they were different from those who wished to carry out the extermination. Anyone not born in the same village or immediate vicinity was met with suspicion and a knife.

She steps out of the house and looks up at a sky full of stars swarming in their burrows as if all was well with the world. Dawn is yet to break. She hurries through the darkness to the turn in the road and looks back. Lamps are burning in all the rooms. This is her refuge and bastion, but looking at it now she feels no belonging or kinship. She took the house in Jerusalem because it reminded her of the one in which she grew up, the family home two days to the north. She felt an immediate pull on the day she came to view it, though nothing remains of that now. The house might as well be an inn. Her attachments are elsewhere.

Only now does she understand the nature of her family and her people. They were created in the image of the Father, of God himself. And because the Father was the God of destruction and vengeance, they became a people of destruction and vengeance. Blood spill led to blood spill like a river to the sea, a deep red sea with the smell of old iron. And then the God, perhaps weary from counting the numbers of the dead, felt compassion for the first time, or something like compassion. He was born among the people to a carpenter and he was put to death. He came to understand that something was missing in the world he had created. A world of plagues and disease, of war and blood lust, of adultery and idolatry and cruelty. He had forgotten to create tenderness. On the cross he became tenderness, and that was how the God of the old stories, the fearsome God of vengeance, would turn the world he had made on its head. He would become the God of compassion towards all things. How could he not?

The birds are up. She can hear them speaking of the troubles to come. The birds are awake and the stars are crawling in the sky as if all was well with the world. She will do the same. She will take her cue from the birds and the stars. She will go on as if nothing were wrong.

She has stops to make, first at the house of Joanna, wife of Chuza, then at the house of Susanna the barren, then Mary, mother of James and Salomé, then Amasa, Leah and Aquila, those women who were her companions when the story came to its sudden end. She stops at each of their dwellings and by the time they reach the dirt road that will take them across the hills to the tomb, there is light in the sky at last. She is at the head of a small group of determined women, those who stayed with him through the hours of agony and followed after, and watched as his body was laid in another man's tomb, and a great stone rolled against the mouth of the cave.

'My children say his miracles are witchcraft,' says Mary, mother of James and Salomé. 'James says a man who works miracles is actually a demon and deserves to be crucified.'

'People say anything, and after all this is your James,' says Amasa. 'We all know what he is like.'

Old Mary remembers the rumours concerning Amasa and James. She says, 'We know what you are like too, Amasa.'

'There are no demons, there are only good angels and bad ones,' says Mary of Magdala. 'And in any case, who will distinguish between angels and demons? Sometimes they disguise themselves to confuse us.'

'Devils have their uses,' says Susanna the barren. 'They are manifestations of God, as much as the sun and the moon and we.'

She points with a dismissive gesture at the lightening sky. The women fall silent as they continue their journey. At last they come to the rise and the silence is broken by whispers. How will they enter the cave? They number only half a dozen. How will they roll away the stone, exhausted as they are from the vigil and the walking? But when they reach the cave they find it open and the stone that barred the entrance rolled to the side. It is no stone but a boulder. Who could have come in the night and moved it?

Confused, suddenly footsore, she goes inside. She is unable to make sense of the picture she has entered. The cave is empty, the rocky ground bare but for a length of stained linen. She lifts it to her face and inhales the smell of blood and fear. He has lain here recently, of that much she is certain. She can feel the warmth of his flesh on the dirty once-white cloth. The Romans, she thinks, the

Romans have taken him. But why would they do such a thing? Or might it have been the twelve, his disciples, the weak and fearful men so trapped in their own skittish fates they did not see the future winging towards them like a giant bird of prey? They saw only their own reflections magnified tenfold. Did they understand the full import of the thoughts he had shared? So many words that had never before been spoken on this earth, words that carried the smell of the new, did they hear? They did not, or they heard something that had not been said. *Once, God was one with you, there was no separation. And the Devil made himself the interpreter of God's language to his people, and all was lost. For the Devil added those falsehoods that set God against his own creation.* How could they hear those words in the way they were meant to be heard and continue as if nothing had changed? They could not, yet they did. They were unaware of the nature of his suffering and the promise it engendered.

She emerges from the tomb to find her companions in a huddle on the ground and she wants to join them, but she will not. To sit down now, at the entrance to this place – she might never get up again. She will keep going and she will not stop. If she stops, she dies. If she dies, he is forgotten. If he is forgotten, all is lost. Led by Susanna, the other women go into the cave to see for themselves that he is gone. Then they set off to Levi's as a group, at a slower pace, hardly speaking, because what is there to say? They stop only once, when Old Mary says she needs a sip of wine 'to make the heart move smoothly, and the feet too'. Saying this, she produces a wineskin from her cloak. They each take a mouthful, which makes the sunlight recede to

11

the edge of her vision. The events of the night seem to have occurred a long time earlier. Her feet move more smoothly, it's true. But her heart does not need the wine. If anything, it beats too fast.

They find Levi with Peter and Andrew at table, the three looking rested and well fed, as if no change had befallen the world. It strikes her that nothing very terrible has happened to them. A man was flayed and crucified on a hill. This is a common occurrence. What can one do? After all, such things happen. Their expressions change – a flinch of the eyes, a hardening around the mouth – when she enters the room and they see that her face is streaked with red dust and tears. They notice that the women have gathered on one side of the table to face them.

'Get up off your throne-chairs,' she says. 'You have no right to feast today.'

Levi says, 'You are in my home, telling me my rights?'

'The Rabbuni is gone. Somebody removed him in the thick of night. Was it you?'

The men admonish her. Peter's voice is the loudest in the room. He considers himself an orator, copying the way the Rabbuni spoke to crowds, expansive and intimate at the same time, as if he were addressing family members or his closest friends. But he cannot make his voice resemble the master's. It grates on the ear like a door that does not fit its hinges. He says she is lying, she has not been to Jesus's tomb – how she marvels at the ease with which the name passes his lips – the body must be there still, where else would it be? He says she is foolish to take *them* for fools, when *they* are his trusted disciples who were with him until the end.

And as if anger is a contagion that spreads from person to person, transmitted by the tone of a voice or a look in the eye, she is angry too. All it takes are the words *trusted disciples* and the contempt in his voice. Suddenly she cannot bear this man. The way he bullies the timid, the way he bullies women, the scent of sweat and something she cannot name, something stale and pungent. Most of all she hates the sound of his voice, the way it changes from ingratiating to rude in a moment, for no reason. So when she speaks, it is in a tone Peter and the men who call themselves disciples have never before heard. She remembers something the master said when they reached the hill, before the taunts of the crowd that lined the road on both sides reduced him to silence. His words return to her now.

'What you see you become,' she says calmly. 'If you see spite, you are spite. If you see Spirit, you are Spirit. If you see the Christ, you become Christ.' Then her own words take over: 'But not you, Peter. You see everything and nothing because you do not see yourself. You *are* everything and nothing. This is why you ran to Galilee – all of you left him and ran when the Romans came.'

There is silence for a moment. Then Old Mary speaks up, the old mother of James whose wine sustained them on the way. It was a great thing to see, she says, the speed at which the men tried to outrun each other, their cries as they fled for their worthless lives. She laughs, a harsh sound in the hushed room. She did not know they could run so fast. Perhaps there was something to be said for cowardice if it put such urgency into a person. But never mind that. It was not running she wanted to talk about. What she wanted to make clear was that the men were not with him at the end, not one of them. They did not see him laid in the cave and it was not they who returned to find him gone. It was the women, only the women.

In the midst of the tumult that follows Old Mary's words, she sees that it is full day and more men have come into the house. She is seized with the knowledge of time passing, never to return. She has never before felt it with such intensity, that time is her enemy, her implacable enemy who will not be appeased. It fills her chest with dread, two fists of dread where her lungs should be. She notices that the voices of the men are raised in mistrust and argument. Levi tells Peter he should visit the sepulchre and confirm the truth of the matter. After some discussion the others agree.

And so it is that Peter will go to the cave and find no body there, no thing except the linen in which they wrapped him. Later, on the next day and the days to come, when they tell the story of the risen body, they will paint themselves as brave men who went to the tomb to see for themselves. They will leave out the story of the woman who was the first to enter the tomb. But they will not be able to erase completely the name of the woman.

She goes back to the cave that evening, alone, with the idea that she might spend the night inside as he had, and that if she stays the whole night she will understand what has happened. But when she gets there she is weary and footsore. She sits at the entrance and covers her face and weeps. Her tears are not tears of helplessness or grief, as some have reported – this is a story with a motif, of the woman who weeps – they are tears of rage. As the sun moves and the light flattens into gold, she goes into the tomb and finds two figures sitting where the body had been, one at the head and one at the feet. Later she will be unable to describe them. Slender or corpulent, rough or well spoken, male or female, she does not know.

'Someone is weeping,' one of them says.

'I wonder why,' says the other, smiling. 'Can someone tell us?'

'I'm not weeping,' she says. 'It's dark in here and your eyes must be playing tricks. In any case it doesn't matter, there are other things to talk about than my tears.'

Then the words come out of her in a rush. She speaks of the importance of objects and of bodies, a tooth, a toe, a twist of beard or a flap of skin, a length of linen stained the colour of rust, because once it held a body that housed a spirit, even if the spirit had now left. She speaks of knowledge and faith, how difficult it is to tell one from the other, how difficult to distinguish spirit from body. So if you know where they have taken him you must tell me, she says, his body belongs to those who loved him. In the gloom their bright eyes laugh at her. Who is she talking about? He must be someone important if she is willing to harangue two innocent strangers.

She says, 'I speak of one whose name you do not know to hear.'

Now she notices a third figure standing to her side, a rough figure slouching slightly. Unlike the smug strangers in white, this man's robe is dusty, as if he has been working many hours in the sun. She thinks it might be the gardener come to tidy up after his exertions, for it is the first day after the Sabbath. Perhaps he took the body away before dawn and has returned to clear the tomb. Who gave him permission, she asks, to move the Rabbuni? Tell her where he is, so she may go and tend to him. The gardener scrutinises her, a look of amusement on his face. She notices that his eyes are too large for his head, shining eyes set prominently in their sockets. He says a familiar word.

'How do you know my name?' she asks.

He makes no reply. Instead he asks questions. Why does she weep? If there is no difference between knowledge and faith, why believe, why not merely apprehend, or perceive without understanding? What use perception if it does not lead to sight? Why does she not see that which is in front of her? Only then does she understand that it is he, changed so much she did not recognise him. Of course he is different. How could he be the same? He has died, as all men die, but now he has returned, as no man does.

'Rabbuni,' says Mary of Magdala.

'Yes.'

'I thought you died.'

'I did die.'

'I thought you died for ever,' she says, embracing him.

'You cannot hold me,' he says, extricating himself. 'I am no longer of those who may be held.'

He lifts his hands and shows her the crusted wounds in his wrists, deep excavations already healing. She wants to kiss the gouges in his flesh. He tells her there is no pain. Sometimes the wounds itch, but he cannot do anything about that. It is as if his limbs no longer belong to him, and this, he says with a laugh, is an unaccustomed, happy feeling. He tells her that some part of him is still in the world, but the smallest, least useful part. Even this will soon pass into light. Then he speaks of different kinds of light. He tells her that bright light is the least conducive, a physical barrier that does not allow the spirit to pass. Half-light is better. And there is always light, even when it is invisible to the eye. He speaks in this way for some time. She does not know how long, because she has no sense of time passing. Her senses are enclosed in the words. He ends by telling her to speak of the things she has seen, because she has witnessed all that happened to him and now she is the first to witness his return. When she speaks of the things she has seen, she must remember to say her name.

This is the book that begins with the end. This is the book that begins with one Mary and ends with another. And because her name has been lost or misplaced or maligned, I say it here:

Mary of Magdala.

# 3

Imagine that the faces looking at you are the faces of children, Mary tells her. What will you say? How will you say it? Shape the truth of what you know in a way they will remember. Keep in mind that they are children and what they want more than anything is to be delighted. Don't think about the words. If you think with your body rather than your mind, the correct words will come. All you have to do is allow them in.

The first time Mary puts her in front of a crowd she forgets everything she has thought to say. She struggles to frame a sentence. She struggles to pronounce her own name. Mary comes up to stand beside her and she knows she must speak now, she must say something, but she grows so dizzy she forgets why she is there. She grips the edge of the table as the ground gives way under her. Slowly the sense of unreality spreads from her feet to her head and beyond, into the branches of the trees and across the false blue of the sky. Mary rescues her. She speaks to the crowd of the mystery of the risen body and of the strangers in the cave. The figure she mistook for a working man. The question she asked. Are you the gardener? And in a way it was the right question, she tells them. He *is* a gardener – of the spirit, making new life from dead earth. At the end of the speech Mary turns to her with a smile. She indicates the crowd and says, Children.

The next day there is a meeting on a mount that has become famous for a sermon he gave there once. This time she prepares herself for the ordeal of speaking. She takes her place and remembers how they waited outside the cave for Mary to emerge, how she went in with the others and saw that he had risen. At that moment time ordinary dissolved into time infinite and she has carried it with her ever since, the knowledge that time may be stretched or shrunk. Time floats. You make of it what you will. It was clear to her then and it is clear to her now as she hears a voice falling around her from another realm, ringing with wisdom, and it takes her a moment to understand that it is her own voice. The faces looking up at her are rapt and bright, the faces of small children.

'The world is a measure of time,' she says, 'and time measures itself in music or language or light. It slows down or speeds up, depending on the nature of the measure it employs. It never ends. For the flesh and the forest the moment of decay must come, when time falls away and the past submits to the future. There is nothing to fear. Death is the beginning, not the end. From death comes that which is eternal. You may see the signs but only if you care to look. The earth at odds with man, man at odds with the animals, the birds in terror for their lives, in terror for us, and above us the sky and its chaos of stars multiplying nightly. What are we to make of it? How do we prepare for the calamity to come?'

She tells them of the soul before ascension, how precarious its state at the moment when it is caught between the world that is ending and the world that is for ever. She tells them of the two figures in the tomb and what they said to Mary. She changes only one part of the story. She does not say the beings were sexless, beyond gender and its limitations. If she does, she knows the men will belittle her account. She will be laughed at, or she will be punished and forced into silence. The figures in the cave were male, she says, and dressed all in white. Angels possibly, but men certainly. Now the old men in the crowd are full of praise. She is the bearer of good news, they cry. Listen to her, she was there, she knows everything. Hallelujah!

But all of that is yet to come. On the evening of the day of the risen Christ, two of the men visit the neighbouring village of Emmaus. As they talk of the events of the week they gesticulate wildly, voices sharp with speculation. From time to time they stop to argue. They do not acknowledge the woman who follows at a distance. There is a hierarchy in the world. The men are true disciples and she is not. Further, she is barren, a woman whose husband left her. They do not see her.

Strange to follow the two and keep a distance, as if she were a servant or suffering from the plague. But Mary has asked her to accompany them to Emmaus. They were not witnesses to the resurrection. All they know is second-hand. She must ensure they speak the truth, even if they are uncertain what that truth may be. She knows what the men say of her, that she is unlucky, born under the wrong star and barren as a blighted field. Why do they assume it was she who was at fault? Why do they not suspect her husband, who married again but is still childless? She'd like to tell them that it is her husband who is the barren one. If she did not have children it is because she willed it that way. She took precautions.

Two weeks after the wedding she knew her husband was a man without magnetism, whose true occupation and pleasure was to enact the same routine each day. His father had come to her family to propose his son as a match. A man among men, her husband's father, who had travelled and seen the world, who wore rings on his fingers and a many-coloured fringed robe, whose eyes, lined with black, seemed to see into her deepest thoughts. She was excited when her family accepted the proposal on her behalf. If the son were anything like the father, they would have a happy life.

But the son was nothing like his father. Her husband's great passion was to start the day with stewed fruits to ensure that his digestion and bowel movements were regular. He insisted on the same meals at the same time. If there was any departure from the scheme he became confused, or angry. He wanted to control everything, what they ate, when, how the food was cooked, how she did the housework, how often or how rarely she was allowed out of the house – everything. Most nights he turned to the wall and fell asleep before she came to bed, and those were pleasant times for her. But he expected her to lie with him once a week, always at night, two days before the Sabbath. The first time they lay together he told her she could not kiss him and rut with him at the same time. This was the word he used, 'rut', as if they were animals. You can kiss me or rut with me, but you cannot do both, he said. You have to choose one or the other. She chose the rutting, because she preferred not to kiss him. What she found most disagreeable about her husband was his smell of the farmyard and the morning mucking-out, for he was an enthusiastic farmer. He smelled of the goats whose company he enjoyed. Sometimes she wondered if he cared more for them than he cared for his wife. When a goat was sick his manner changed in a way that seemed strange to those who knew him. He lost interest in his food. When she was sick he seemed hardly to notice. She came to see that they had nothing in common. Nothing about him pleased her.

It was she who suggested that since she was unable to give him heirs, he might think of marrying again. Look at the goats, she told him, if a nanny is unable to conceive we replace her with another. When it comes to child-bearing and rearing, we are not so different from the animals. You deserve to have children, she said, it is your right. He did nothing about it for a year, and she knew why. He did not want to change his living arrangements. A new wife would overturn the well-established routine, the work duties, his savings. It wasn't worth the trouble. When at last he decided to leave her and marry again, she felt only elation, mixed with her usual caution. She wants to tell the two men and the others who talk about her that the barrenness that visited her married life was a blessing. But this is something a woman cannot say.

The men pass the outskirts of the city and stop at a culvert by the gates. They are talking to a slender man of familiar mien. She stands to the side of the road and listens. The man asks why they walk abroad on a fine day, crying to the heavens, sighing and shouting as if someone in their house had died. One of the two, whose name she has forgotten, asks if the man is a stranger to Jerusalem that he does not know what has happened.

The man says, 'Tell me, Cleopas, what has happened?'

'Today some women went to the sepulchre of the Christ and found no sign of him. So some of us went to see for ourselves,' says Cleopas. 'But wait, how do you know my name?'

The stranger says he knows many names. He takes a slow breath and enumerates the prophets going back to Moses, names known, unknown and forgotten, names from the recent past and from so long ago that their stories have acquired the stability of myth. He talks of seven female prophets, Miriam amongst them, who stood against Moses her brother and suffered the displeasure of the Lord. He quotes passages from the scriptures that speak of the prophets and the coming of the Christ, and of the death of Christ in confirmation of the prophecies from the time of Samson, whose death, too, was fully conscious and fully expected. He reminds them that the Christ had been offered wine before his death and he refused, without hesitation he refused. Did they not wonder why? Which man would not wish to dull the pain of a mortal wound? This simple act of refusal brings an important question. Should the Christ have suffered or should he have elected not to suffer?

Confused by the unexpected turn the conversation has taken, the two men fall silent.

'You foolish fellows,' says the stranger, 'you slow of heart, you half-heart halfwits to believe not the prophets and the women who are prophets. I ask you again for the last time, should the Christ not have suffered as he did? Don't think, speak!'

The men stare at him in bewilderment.

She answers because she knows him now. 'If the Son suffered and died as the prophets prophesied, he did as was willed by God his father.'

'At last. Someone who knows,' says the Christ, looking to the heavens and then at her. He beckons her to join them. Then he asks the men, 'Now do you know the correct answer?'

The men squint at the sun, which is high in the sky. They squint long enough that they are blinded. When they look at the stranger he is a figure of light, an orb of bright blue sky. Now the orb strolls along the road and where it goes, they follow.

The orb says, 'Oh, you magnificent nothings! You voids of the void! You captains of folly! Listen to the woman. All that the Son did was willed. Try and remember it, which you won't. Report it correctly, which you can't. I know all this, yet I waste my breath. Why?'

By now they have reached Emmaus and the two men are eager to find an inn and wash the dust from their feet. When the stranger makes to walk on, he who spoke so knowledgeably about the prophets and insulted them so congenially, they ask that he join them for supper. He says he would be happy to do so but only if their sister will join them too. She is an outcast woman from a neighbouring town, they tell him. A barren woman whose husband has left her.

'And what of it? Open your eyes and listen. Open your ears and see.'

24

People will see us together, say the men.

'Good. By joining us she honours us.'

He seats the woman at the head of the table and takes his own place last, at the centre. The way he sits, the way he holds the bread and hesitates before he eats, the men know him as the Christ. There is something in him they have not seen before. A lightness of manner, as if the worst is behind him and the path ahead is easeful, where before all was worry and fear. They want to tell him that they know him now, but when they look for him, his seat is empty. It is as if he had never been there. The taste of the meat becomes ashes in their mouths.

They return to Levi's house, she following at a distance, and they describe the risen Christ, what he was wearing, what he said, how mirthful he was, joking with them, insulting them in a light-hearted way, or at least they thought it was light-hearted. As they speak he appears in their midst in the same position at the centre of the table. He terrifies them. A ghost, they say, a ghost is among us. She is standing to the side because she has not been invited to join them. Now she steps forward. Look, she says, showing them the shattered bones of his feet and the deep punctures in his wrists.

'No ghost is made of flesh and bone.'

Even this small gesture, the upturning of his palms and the baring of his feet, this small exertion seems to tire him. He asks for meat. Someone brings cooked fish and a piece of honeycomb. He eats slowly, remarking that honey is a salve for everything except the open wounds of crucifixion. Some among them laugh at this joke, but quietly, as if they are unwilling to laugh in his presence. He tells them that

25

his death had been ordained a long time earlier. He was reluctant at first. Who would not have been? But in the end he did his Father's bidding, as the prophets foretold. After the meal they leave the house and walk out of the village. A cool night. There is a scent in the air of wild thyme or hyssop. They walk slowly to make the evening last. He stops beside an almond tree and picks up something fallen in the dust. She makes out a handful of white flowers.

'You must allow the women to speak,' he says quietly, as if only to himself. 'But you won't. I can see it in your stubborn eyes.'

'Which women?' one of the men asks. 'And why must they speak?'

'Because if not for them, my teaching would amount to nothing. Mary of Magdala, and Mary and Martha of Bethany, and Susanna, and Joanna, and the other women who provided for me out of their resources – without them I could not have continued.'

As he says the name Bethany they find that they have reached the village of the same name, and they see that he is blessing them, and they understand that he is leaving. They will do as he says. They will speak of what they have seen and they will follow his instructions, all except one. With the passing of time the elders of the Church will ignore or forget his teaching with respect to women. They will build the Church on the witness of the women but they will refuse to record their names.

But this they cannot change, that the risen Christ appeared first to Mary of Magdala and that it was the women who were the first leaders of the Church. This is the book of the martyrdom of Jesus, and this is the book of the women who travelled with him. This is the story that goes backwards to Eve and her fearful companion Adam, who wished for the fruit of the tree of knowledge but lacked the courage to pluck it.

And this is the story of Susanna the Barren.

# 4

In the narrow walkways of the town, made narrower by the mob, food and mucus are smeared on the wall. On the ground, pellets of goat shit that stick to her sandals. She can feel their vile insults like spit on her skin. The filth that spews even from the women, even from the young. She knows the abuse is aimed at him, not her, but they are close together. The women are trying to shield him. They are all targets. Sometimes she catches a glimpse of a face in the crowd, mouth twisted into a kind of smile, voice thick and lost to reason. She wonders at their fury. What has he done to them, what unforgivable wrong? He must have injured them in some way for hatred so naked. But he has not, she knows, he has done nothing except offer kindness. Then why are they eager to see him tortured unto death? She sees their mouths moving, but cannot hear their cries among the frenzy of the mob. She looks in their eyes, wide open, like small wounds in the stretched skin of the face. Then she knows why they hate him. Kindness is a taunt to those who love cruelty.

Near the Damascus Gate where the crowd is thicker Old Mary recognises a woman she knows from the temple. The woman is with an older man and a small child. Something about them catches her eye, the air of excitement and the gleam on their faces and the feast clothes they are wearing. The woman's skin is shiny with sweat, as if she has been cooking all morning, or lying with the man in a field, or running so that she won't be late for the entertainment. The thrill and rare spectacle of a man crucified. Her new clothes, the child's freshly washed hair, the air of festivity that surrounds the three, none of it prepares Old Mary for what follows. The woman pushes roughly through the crowd while the man and child stand to one side. When she gets to the front the woman waits until he is directly before her, until he turns to look at her, and then she spits full in his eyes. On her way back to her family the spitting woman sees Old Mary. Their eyes meet and it is the look on the woman's face that Mary will not forget. The spitting woman glows with energy, alive with the triumph of what she has done, this woman who seemed so mild when they met at the temple, always so accommodating and reasonable, with whom she has shared some of her worries about her illness and her anxiety about her son.

It makes her wonder about the people she knows, men and women whose true natures emerge only inside the mob, who come to life only when they are borne aloft by others and set free. It makes her wonder about her own children, her James and Salomé. She knows instantly that if by some evil chance she finds one of them in the mob, it will be James, waiting impatiently for the smell of spilled blood, a shine on his face as repulsive as the spitting woman's. He had been a tender-hearted boy who became a cold and distant man. For some time now he has never addressed her except in anger. Everything she does irritates him, even the food she prepares, even her clothes, which he thinks too shabby, and her hair, which he says is unkempt. Most of all he resents her for being under the spell of the man he calls 'your Galilean'. He does not like that she uses her wealth to help him. My Galilean, she thinks, enjoying the sound of it. She could not understand her son's anger and she asked him outright what bothered him about the Christ, a man who has harmed nobody. What has he done to you? Her son looked at her as if she were a stranger he had encountered at the fish market.

'He is not one of us,' he said, 'he is from outside.' Then he left the room and refused to say more.

*From outside*, but outside of where? If Galilee was outside, which place was not? In that case, she was from outside the moment she wandered beyond the city limits of Jerusalem – and so was her son. Were they never to leave the confines of the small town, the narrow street, the familiar house in which they had always lived? Is that what it meant to be on the inside? If this was the world that was on its way, she was pleased not to be a part of it.

Shortly after they pass the Damascus Gate, not long after the woman spits on him, he falls to his knees and tries to get up, but cannot. Perhaps, like an ordinary man, he has reached the end of his endurance. She cannot imagine such a thing. She knows he hasn't taken a morsel since supper at the home of Simon the Pharisee. He hasn't slept. He's been questioned all night and scourged at dawn, the blood still crusting on his skin. It's no surprise that the weight of the cross-beam is too much for him. When he falls, she and the other women try to help but they are not allowed to,

30

and some among them begin to weep – Amasa and Leah and Joanna – out of frustration as much as sorrow. But Aquila, who is the youngest, does not. And Mary of Magdala does not. Dry-eyed, her face a mask, she tells them to hide their tears. Witnesses to a crucifixion are allowed to ridicule and mock but they are not allowed to weep. This is the rule, says Mary, and there is a reason for it.

'They wish to outlaw any sign of sympathy. If you make a display of your kindness they will persecute you. Keep your distress to yourself, they are watching.'

Old Mary tries, but her tears have a life of their own. It has always been that way. If she tries not to cry, it is certain the tears will come. Soon she'll be wailing. And what of it? She is an unremarkable old woman whose life is nearing its remarkable end. Without being aware of it or desiring it, she had been swept up in the great story of her time, the single most important thing that happened to her, beside which the facts of her life are insignificant. Her marriage and widowhood, her time as a housewife and mother. Now she is at the end, witness to a murder she could not have foreseen. She looks him in the eyes and weeps.

'Daughter of Jerusalem,' he whispers, because he doesn't want the soldiers to hear, 'weep not for me but for yourself and your children. If they do these things in a green tree, what shall be done in the dry?'

Wind gusts into her face the rich smell of rain. She imagines trees that bubble into kindling, a small flame that spreads to other trees until the hillside is on fire, spreading, spreading, until the hillsides all are burning, hundreds of fires that together create an inferno, a beast that will swallow the land, the ocean, the sky. Her vision lit by flames, she

31

is brought back to the moment by the sound of blows. One of the soldiers is kicking him to his feet. When that doesn't work, the man tries mockery. You are the King of the Jews, are you not? You walk on water, do you not? What are you waiting for? Do it now, get up and walk. If you are a king, surely you can rise? Surely you can do this small thing, O great, O most powerful king of the world? To each question, he makes the same reply: 'So say you.' Is it exhaustion or insolence that makes him speak so quietly? So say *you*, one of the soldiers repeats in a singsong voice, mocking him, stretching out the last syllable as if he were praying. They try again to drag him to his feet but he is held to the ground by the cross-beam.

Because he is unable to rise, the soldiers take hold of a man who happens to be passing, who says his name is Simon of Cyrene. He cannot refuse when they tell him to carry the beam. Falling in beside the Christ and the women, he sees the crowds lining the way and he smells the hysteria. The cross-beam is a dead weight that has already put splinters in his hands. He moves slowly, his eyes on the ground. Old Mary is not sure he can be trusted. What if the Romans and the Jewish elders have put him there and instructed him to be friendly? What if his true mission is to report what they say? What if they are all arrested and murdered as an example to the people? She realises she has never thought this way before, calmly suspicious of strangers. She blames Mary of Magdala for her new knowledge of the ways of men.

The wind picks up, flinging sand in circles around the street. She spits to the side and wipes her face with her hands and puts her fingers into her tangled grey hair to dislodge the grit. Then the wind starts up in earnest and a dust storm whips around her ears. She shields her eyes with her veil but the sand finds its way into her clothes and hair. The women huddle together and wait for the storm to pass, their eyes squeezed shut, veils tight around their heads. The soldiers form a ring around the Christ. They know nothing about the man they are punishing, she thinks. They do not know that he has no wish to escape. More than they, it is he who wants to see this story through to its bloody, mythic end. It is clear to her that no one is more complicit in the death of Jesus than Jesus himself. When the storm dies down a little the soldiers push on. She stumbles and grabs blindly for Mary of Magdala, and the two women walk steadily against the wind. Then, as suddenly as it began, the storm falls out and all is as before. There is no sign of its passing but a film of sand that covers the city.

This is when she sees the birds, dozens of mockingbirds and sunbirds and birds she does not know the names of, small knots of feathers dropped on the road around her. She picks one up. Soft and dust-coloured, small as her thumb and already stiffening, its wire claws point at the sky. By her feet she sees more small bundles, a wash of them, and this is another terrible thing on a day of terrible things, unimaginable occurrences, bitter omens of catastrophe. Birds fallen dead from the sky! She puts the creature down with its claws facing to the side. Then, shivering, she joins the other women.

She feels herself moving between the world she has always known, the clean edges of things that have been a part of her life since she was a child, and the world that is to come, a world of fear that blots out the sunlight. When she was young, her father would tell her about other lands, that the earth was a vast place and its exact dimensions could only be imagined, that nobody knew how deep the oceans went or how high the sky. Today, on a day when she has gone further into the world than she ever thought possible, she senses her father reaching out to her in the shape of hands made of sand, a storm figure seeking to embrace her. At the last moment, just as it seemed he would touch her after hours and years of reaching, he falls to the ground and breaks into particles, a film of dust, or a handful of dead feathers flung from the sky.

When they reach the hill and the hammering begins, she loses all sense of herself. Hours must have passed. The light has leaked out of the evening. She sees that they have nailed the cross-beam to a plank of timber already planted in the ground. They position his limbs as if they are handling a suit of clothes. He does not struggle or cry out. He offers no resistance. And so it is over quickly, the roping of his arms to the cross. Her vision brightens and she feels she is coming up with a fever. Against the promise she made to herself, she looks away when the first nail is hammered into the small of his wrist, his slender wrist that will shred against the iron before long. She looks away and her thoughts roam where they will and for some reason she remembers the Canaanite.

She was ten or nine. She and her sister were playing at the front of the house when the man approached. Their favourite game, rolling a wooden lion past the gates of a city they had made out of stones. The lion stood on a board attached to big wooden wheels and as he rolled down the small main street of the town the townspeople screamed in terror. Some among them did not scream but surrendered

34

meekly, as if to a new god. She was so engrossed that she did not look up when the visitor shuffled past. All she noticed was that his feet were cracked at the heels, cracks so deep they might have been made with a butcher's knife, and that he was told to come to the back of the house. She stopped playing lion and went inside. Her father stood impassively at the back porch, staring at the visitor. The man sat in the noon sun, near their fields of white barley, his eyes on the meal he had been given. He was eating from a plate her family did not use. She asked why the man had not been welcomed into the house, and her father explained that he was a Canaanite. She asked him what that meant and her father said, He is the slave of slaves. She looked carefully at the man. It would show on his face, she thought. His condition would show in his eyes or his nose. There would be markings and ceremonial slave scars. His hair would be unusual, and his skin, and his manner of speaking and eating. But she could see no difference between him and her father, except that her father's clothes were finer and his skin fairer. Otherwise they could have been cousins. Before the man left, her father took a pitcher of water to him and the man cupped his hands and drank. He washed his face and thanked them for the food and left as silently as he had come.

For some reason she remembers him now, the Canaanite, as she hears a sound like the splintering of wood and looks up to see a soldier driving a long square nail into the sweet bones of his feet. Grunts of pleasure from the Romans and Jews scattered about the hillside. They have been waiting for this moment. Their faces, like the face of the woman from the temple, are unremarkable in every way except one. They know to hide the emotion that fills them. She wonders if there will come a day when those who believe only in the rule of the sword, in destroying the outsider and the stranger, will give up their power over those who believe in kindness? Otherwise why does he suffer on the cross, and what meaning is there in his death? She hears the grunts of pleasure and cries of shame and anguish from those who are gathered at the base of the cross. Dizzy, she tilts her head and looks up, and notices that his lips are moving. What is he saying? She hears the name Mary but it is not she who is being addressed.

She is Old Mary, mother of James and Salomé.

# 5

Tell them the day comes that will burn as an oven, write, Mary, that the monuments they raise will be heaps of broken stone, and the flood will come again, and even as the days to come will burn you, even as the last bird in the last sky burns, even in the days of burning so shall you drown, and no ark may hold you from the whiteness that floats upon the earth, as a kiss in a poisoned chalice, the burning flood that leaves neither root nor branch, neither sweet fruit nor green leaf, neither air to breathe nor light in the sky, and to the mighty that raise their monuments to the heaven, I say woe unto you and woe to your city that is exalted unto heaven, for it will be brought to hell, woe to you whose flight is in winter and woe if you flee in the summer, woe be thy name, woe is thy reward and true birthright, for when the end begins you shall be first brought down, you shall be first among the beguiled, you, the well-spoken, the wealthy, the greed-hungry, who will flock together in fear, and some will come in my name and praise the Father, but believe them not, for they do the work of Satan while speaking the word of the Lord in their white vestments and their gibberish and their temples of money, tell them they shall be brought down, and for all that they seduce you to war they shall be brought down, and for all that they use the word of false gods they shall be brought down, and for all that they say, pitting one tribe against another, high against low, tell them they shall be brought down, and those that take sides for one colour against another, the brawlers with the yellow hair, the one whose horses are many, the one who bathes in the blood of the murdered, the one who sings with the tongue of the hateful, they shall be brought down, and the time will come when nations of migrants will rise against nations of migrants, when brother will betray brother, and the father will betray the son, and the child will betray the parent, when friends are slain for water, and the oiled voice of he who trades in fear will be heard above all others, but your voice too shall be heard in the courts of men, Mary, inside the moving air and on the byways where rumours live, in the north where ice melts the sick sap of ages and in the south where fires rage among the living and the dead, and when that time is come do not fear what must be done, let your heart lead your voice lead your fist and the hour's yours, for that is the day of burning and water, and he that is on the housetop should not go into the house or enter therein, and if you are in the field do not turn back to your house to collect your belongings, for your belongings are no longer yours, as your children are no longer yours, and the day is come when you will say, blessed is the womb that cannot bear and blessed the breast that cannot give suck, for these are the days of affliction and this is the time of dread, when lamentation is upon the land, and she who has eyes to read will understand my words, two hundred or two thousand years from me.

# 6

She has swept up the leaves in the courtyard into three
shedding piles. She is about to clear them when there is a
noise at the gate. A crowd armed with staves and knives
and rocks, and at the head of the group her master, Caiaphas.
The crowd moves in stops and starts, forming and
re-forming, breaking apart and coming together elsewhere.
Secret faces are exposed for a moment, safe in their oneness.
The three piles of leaves are trampled and scattered across
half the courtyard. She presses herself against the wall,
wondering at the reason for such commotion. But as the
mob makes its way into the main house she notices a slender
man on whom they have laid hands. It seems to her that
he has no intention of escaping. If anything he is the only
one among them who is not agitated. His nut-brown skin
and weather-beaten hands give him the look of someone
who has spent years outdoors in all kinds of rough accom-
modation, someone unaccustomed to the life her master
enjoys. Then she notices a wild-haired boy pushing his way
into the crowd. He is bare-chested, his face streaked, and
he stands absolutely still in the midst of the uproar. With
a small flourish he takes off the piece of dirty linen wrapped

around his waist and puts it on the slender man's shoulders. Naked, the boy walks away slowly and disappears into a crowd of men milling near the gates. She reminds herself to tell Bilhah about the mad naked boy. It started off as a normal day, she thinks. How strange it has become.

Later that evening, in the small hours of the morning, and until the end of her life, the question she will be asked most often is about the man set upon by the mob. What was he wearing? Did he seem frightened or resigned? Was he very different in appearance from the men who held him captive – he must have been, after all? Years later, far removed from the event, the questions will become more outlandish. What colour were his eyes? Is it true one was brown and the other black? Could it be that it was all an act and they let him go and a lookalike died in his place? Around his head was there a blue light or was it the colour of anointing oil?

After a while she will give the same set of replies. He was thin, with dark brown skin and a short black beard and goodly eyes. He didn't seem frightened but relieved, as if he was happy to be arrested and looking forward to whatever punishment they had planned. All of which is true. But she will say other things she is less sure about, and in time she will be unable to remember whether these things happened or if she imagined them. Was there really a glow around him that was so bright there was no need of torches? When the boy put the dirty linen on him, the length of cloth that looked like he had spent many nights sleeping in a field, did it really cleanse itself? Did contact with the man's brown skin change the nature of the linen? As if it had been washed by a very careful servant, someone more careful than she was? And was there blood on his mouth from the beating he received, but as he went past her, or was pushed past her, the blood seemed to disappear? Did it happen that way? She isn't sure and she will be less sure as the years pass.

When most of the mob has gone into the main house she notices a straggler skulking outside, unsure whether to go in with the others or stay where he is. Muttering urgently to himself, he paces back and forth with his chest puffed out and his hands balled into fists. He seems afraid to approach. Yet when he gazes at the house and the rowdy men around it his face is full of longing. You can come in, she tells the straggler. Don't be frightened. It won't cost you anything.

The windows of the house are open and she can hear raised voices from inside, the voice of the master louder than the others. She runs into the maidservants' quarters to tell Bilhah what has happened. Her friend is feeding small logs into the cauldron fire to heat water for the master's bath. She describes the naked boy with the dirty hair who took off his only item of clothing. She talks about the man the master has arrested and the mob that seems to hate him. He must have done something terrible, she says. He must have murdered someone or stolen an ox. No, Bilhah replies, he didn't kill or steal. He is from the north country, a town called Nazareth. His father is a carpenter.

'Does that mean he is a poor man?'

'Yes, poor like you and me.'

'Is that why they arrested him, because he is poor?'

'Yes, and because his friends are fisherfolk and thieves and women.'

'Women – what kind of women?'

'Women like you and me.'

'Is that why they arrested him, because his followers are women?'

'Yes, and because he is poor. They are afraid of the poor. They are afraid of us.'

'Afraid of women?'

'Terrified of women.'

'But why are you crying, Bilhah?'

'I don't know. I don't think the master will bathe now. I feel there's a fog in my head, or is it smoke from the fire?'

Bilhah looks down at her hands, smiling dreamily, and starts to remove some of the logs. As always, she is struck by Bilhah's eyes and the emotions she sees in them: sadness, but also compassion and puzzlement and exhaustion.

'Never mind the fire. We can start it again later.'

'They won't let him go, the poor man. He will be put to death.'

And seeing her friend in tears, she is sad too, though she does not know why. It might be the events of the day, the men with the staves and knives, the mad naked boy, the man who has been arrested, the silent man of Nazareth who will soon be killed – all of it melds together in her head with her friend's tired eyes. She wants to take Bilhah into the courtyard so they can warm themselves by the fire.

'He said it's easier for a camel to enter into the eye of a needle than for a rich man to enter into heaven.'

'Oh. Are there no rich men in heaven?'

'And he said it is easier for a woman to enter heaven than for a man.'

'Bilhah! What if they hear?'

*

Inside the house Caiaphas asks for a witness against the man who calls himself Christ, but there is no one who will come forward. He goes to the scribes and to some among the priests. Witness, he says, who among you will witness? A few men from the crowd join them as they confer in low voices in a corner of the main room. At Caiaphas's signal the guards bind the prisoner's hands behind his back and point at him their spears. Someone slaps him, playfully at first, and then others follow in earnest and the sound of their slaps echoes against the vaulted ceilings. The prisoner's head sinks to his chest. You see, says Caiaphas, everything moves towards the end of the story and you cannot stop it. Tell me, who among you will be a witness? He shuffles to the front of the room and takes his seat on a dais lined with brass altars and lamps.

A man comes forward.

'Who are you?' says Caiaphas, adjusting his bulk on the chair. His calves and soft fat feet are sore from marching in procession through the streets of the town.

'Silas the baker,' says the man.

He swears that the man who calls himself Christ said he would destroy the temple with his own hands. He made the promise while he was destroying another temple where he threw out the moneylenders whose livelihoods he tried to ruin, and did ruin, though not for long. They were back at their spots soon enough. For how can we function without them? It is impossible to conduct a business without the help of moneylenders. The baker knows this as truth.

Another man comes forward to dispute the baker's version. In fact, he heard the Christ say he would destroy all temples that had been built with hands and he would raise a temple built with no hands, greater than any temple seen by man. And in this temple there would be no priests, no moneylenders, no scribes, only those who worship the Lord. The man said it. The witness heard with his own two ears. At this the men assembled in the front of the room begin to shout insults at the prisoner.

'Be quiet,' Caiaphas says, trying to make himself comfortable on the hard seat. He wants a cushion for his aching buttocks.

A third man comes forward to dispute the second man's version. He heard the prisoner say something much more dangerous, that should put the fear and the great anger into the hearts of the elders. The prisoner said any type of temple was a site for pagans, a place for adultery and gossip. He said the temple was a marketplace for usurers. He said the priests were the worst creators of these sins, particularly the sin of pride. The only temples without sin were the houses of the poor. Those were his words exactly. The witness swears that he saw the prisoner say this, saw it with his own two eyes.

Three witnesses, each better than the last. Caiaphas decides this is enough to bring about a quick end to the trial. It has been a long day. He is in need of a bath and a hot meal. He imagines the tender ministrations of his maid-servants and his wife. It is time to ask the question that will bring the trial to a close.

'The Sanhedrin asks the prisoner, to whom do you pray?'

There is no reply from the bound man.

'Have you nothing to say to those who are witness against you?'

The man's head lifts towards a window set high into the wall. But the sky outside is dark and no light falls into the room.

The two maidservants climb onto the stone porch at the far side of the courtyard. Together they have quickly cleared the leaves. But there is more to be done and they cannot do it until the crowd has gone. They have put some of the heated water into a basin for the master. He likes to wash his hands before he sits down with his jug. He likes to drink before he eats. Usually he drinks a lot and eats very little. The evening has turned cold and the torches have been lit. The courtyard fire is roaring and someone has lit another near the far porch. Her eyes take some time to adjust to the darkness outside the firelight and to the figures that populate the darkness. She notices the straggler sitting with his back to the flames. He stares out into the night as if he is waiting for someone. The back of his tunic is stained with mud or wine, she isn't sure which. When he turns to the fire to warm his hands, Bilhah recognises him.

'I remember you. Weren't you one of those who were with the man they arrested, Jesus of Nazareth?'

'I don't know anything,' Peter says quickly.

She isn't sure if he is angry or frightened.

Bilhah, annoyed by his outburst, says, 'You must know something. Everybody does. For example, don't you know how to catch a fish? And isn't it just as easy to catch a man as it is to catch a fish?' Then, lowering her eyes and her voice, 'He healed my mother from the sleeping sickness. They should not have arrested him.'

'I don't know him. And neither do I understand a word of what you are saying.'

'You don't know him.'

'No. I don't know him. How many times must I say the same thing?'

'I saw you with him. Aren't you one of the disciples?'

Peter gets up and leaves the fire. He walks some way into the night and waits in the cold. Above him the stars are out in their thousands and the moon is nowhere to be seen. He puts his hands together and his lips appear to move but she cannot hear what he is saying.

The high priest wants his bath and he wants supper. Neither comfort seems close at hand. The elders are still talking among themselves in their reedy, self-important old men's voices. He is sick of old men. He has had to involve his father-in-law in this business, Annas, who was high priest before him. And his father-in-law must be the least amenable old man in all of Israel. If not on all the earth. When he first went to meet him with a proposal to marry his daughter, his future father-in-law refused. He said Caiaphas was 'far below' the station his daughter enjoyed in life. Annas agreed only after other pressure had been brought to bear, namely the lure of the shekels left to Caiaphas by his own father. That morning he had sent the man who called himself Christ, who called himself the Messiah, to his father-in-law. He had hoped Annas would make the decision for him and condemn the man to death. But the wily old man had simply interrogated the prisoner and escorted him back to his son-in-law's house. And now the weight of the decision was upon him once again.

The elders announce they will confer some more. They are deciding a man's life, more witnesses must be produced. The word is sent into the crowd and quickly a man comes forward to say that he saw the prisoner speaking in tongues. It happened in Cana. Everyone has heard about the incident when the prisoner used sorcery or trickery to remove the evil spirits from one who had died. The dead man came clawing out of the ground, his face and body wound with the muddy burial clothes, dead flesh crawling with filth. The witness's own eyes saw this Jesus whispering to the man, and so he moved closer, and what he heard had shocked him, shocked him so much he could barely repeat it now. Tell us what you heard, says the Sanhedrin. All manner of spells, the witness continues. Incantations that made the newly risen dead man roll his eyes into his skull, knee-deep in the disturbed soil of his grave, confused about everything he was forced to undergo, but most of all about why he had been made to return to a world he was happy enough to leave. The witness heard the spells with his own ears. He is here tonight to report what happened, a report he has made faithfully and without prejudice.

Caiaphas asks Jesus, 'What do you say to the witness of this man who saw what you did in Cana?'

The prisoner takes a breath and for a moment it seems that he has decided to reply at last, but then he changes his mind.

What a day it has been, a day like no other, unending, and more people than she has ever seen going in and out of the house. She is on the porch and she can hear the master's questions issuing one after the other from inside, those cruel questions with no correct answer. She thinks: the prisoner is doing the right thing by not replying. Whatever he says will be the end of him. However carefully he chooses his words, their wrath will descend on him and destroy him. If she peers into the window she catches glimpses of the master and the prisoner, and the soldiers and elders. There is a moment when she is sure the prisoner looks out and sees her. He sees the straggler who has returned to the fire. She knows him now, the straggler. His smallness of stature and the anxious set of his shoulders. The way his hands are always bunched into fists to defend himself from invisible attackers. Sometimes he mutters and sometimes he laughs. Bilhah sees him too, and says to the others by the fire that he is one of the twelve followers. The straggler denies it. But you must be among his friends, says Bilhah. Your accent and manner are Galilean. Why don't you admit it? The straggler curses the day and the hour that have brought him to this house. He was looking only to come in out of the cold night air. He saw the crowd and followed. He has no idea who she is talking about. Why won't she leave him alone? Then he falls silent. It is late now and dark. She does not know what time it is exactly but it must be very late, or early, because the cock crows once and then again. For some reason the straggler begins to weep.

Inside, Caiaphas says, 'Are you the Christ?'
    And at last there is an answer from the bound man.
    'Even if I tell you, you won't believe me.'
    'Are you the Son of God?'
    'If you say so, so must I be.'

48

At this the high priest is so frustrated at the man's composure, and so angry at his own lack of skills as an interrogator, that he pulls at the sleeve of his ephod. It comes apart at the shoulder seam. His heavy eyes gorge on the tear in the fabric. The pig-set eyes roll in the sweating sockets and he sits heavily on the seat that has served him for the years of judgement. Pushing downwards: the gorged bull buttocks. Straining into coherence: the sentence.

'You heard him. You heard the words from his own sly mouth. We need no more witnesses. Condemn the prisoner. The prisoner is condemned.'

She and Bilhah are standing at their spot in the courtyard when the mistress calls from inside. She wants to know what the master is doing now. Is he still questioning the Galilean? How much longer will Caiaphas take to settle the sorry business? But the mistress will not come out into the throng of unwashed strangers. She hates that they are using her house like a thoroughfare. She wants Bilhah by her side.

'Are you coming?' says Bilhah.

'In just a moment.'

She should go in too. There will be more work for her. More water must be fetched, livestock tended, meals served and utensils cleaned. But she stays where she is and looks up at the overcast sky. Small raindrops arrive on the wind. A moment ago the night was clear and now the stars are invisible, hidden behind thick sheets of iron. Suddenly the whole night feels like a dream filled with the sound of blows and cries and marked by blood spatter. She hopes she will wake up soon.

She is alone by the courtyard wall when they bring the prisoner out. The man from Nazareth is bound and blindfolded. There is blood on his clothes and a streak of spittle in his hair. Someone pulls off the blindfold and pushes him from behind. He falls lightly to his knees. When he looks up, she sees the bruises around his eyes. The straggler is nowhere to be found. The noise of the mob, the things they are saying, the blows, it makes her want to turn her eyes. Now she understands why Bilhah could not watch any more of their cruelty. It is like watching a child being tortured. They are dragging the man from Nazareth into the street when she notices some women following at a distance. A small group of five or six silent women. Where have they come from? As a possible answer takes shape in her head, she steps forward to join them.

This is her chapter and this is her name:

Aquila the maidservant.

# 7

She knows about the fame that precedes him or follows him wherever he goes. It visits the houses he visits and the objects he touches, and those men and women who are closest to him. It stays long after he has gone. It gives the names of unremarkable places a new quality. Now, when someone speaks of Nazareth or Galilee, she hears something that was not there before. The places associated with him are changed by his fame. She knows this because it happened the first time he visited their village and her sister Martha opened the doors of the house to him. Martha who is older, and louder because she is older, took charge as she liked to do. Breathlessly she issued commands. Heat the water. Prepare the table. Send to the baker for more bread. Send for wine. Change your clothes.

She obeyed as many of her sister's instructions as she could and she forgot everything when he started to speak. He was replying to one of the fishermen who followed him around, a disciple who wouldn't stop talking about the buildings he had seen in a town they visited the day before.

'Wonderful, just wonderful!' the disciple kept saying. 'What manner of stones! What manner of buildings! The temple steps, the forecourt, the beauty of the construction! I don't have the words to describe them.'

'You just did,' said one of the others.

'No, no,' said the man. 'Yesterday I saw wonders I cannot render with my tongue.'

He seemed thunderstruck by buildings she thought unremarkable. She had seen so many of them she no longer noticed. Not so the poor fisherman, whose wonder was infinite (someone, you would think, who'd seen a few wondrous sights in his time – for example, a man walking on water, for example, fishes multiplying before his eyes – but no, a few buildings and he was speechless).

The Christ in his reply used half the words the disciple had used. He used the simplest of words and because his words were plain the effect was greater. There was nothing gentle about what he said. Later, when she heard people talk about what a gentle person he was, she would correct them. No, he was not, she would insist. Pay attention to what he said. *Think not that I am come to send peace on earth. I did not come to bring peace, but a sword.* Those are not the words of someone being gentle. He wasn't interested. He didn't have the time.

That day, he told the fisherman that no stone would remain upon another and no building would stay standing. Beautiful or ugly, all would fall. The tallest buildings would be first to be crushed into dust. She was so affected by the sound of his voice that she forgot the chores her sister had set for her. She shouted her agreement without fully understanding what he had said. Yes, she cried. She went into the room to sit at his feet, the only woman who had dared to do so. By sitting at his feet she was proclaiming that she too was a disciple equal to any of the fishermen.

Martha began to complain. 'Master, my sister has left me to do all the work. Should she not help me when there is so much to be done?'

'Let her be. Mary chose correctly.'

That was all he said and it was enough. Martha left the room and a silence grew. She sensed that the men were made uncomfortable by her presence. To add to their discomfort, she decided to speak.

'When the buildings are ground into dust what will become of us?'

'If the buildings are destroyed what will happen to the people inside, is that what you are saying?'

'Yes.'

'Can no one answer this woman's good question?'

The men shrugged. There were grunts of amusement. He had talked about the future before, but he had described so many scenarios they were confused as to which one applied to the present question. Also they were tired, having drunk too much wine, which by no means was a rare condition for fishermen.

She said, 'Will we also be ground down into dust?'

One of the men slumped to the floor. Almost immediately she heard him snoring. It's happening, she thought. At long last it is happening. I am speaking with the Christ, speaking with him in my own house.

'What do you think is the answer to your question?'

'When we die we fall, like buildings.'

'Yes,' said the Christ, 'and there you will stay until the Lord returns to raise you into new life, a life that will not end all of a sudden for the meanest of reasons. Becoming dust is not something to be concerned about. Dust cannot feel or rue the passage of time, dust is insensible, which means it is at peace. So whether your experience lasts a moment or a hundred years, it does not matter.'

These are the things she remembers from his first visit.

Long after he has gone, the people of their village and strangers from nearby towns come to the gate to look at the house. Such is the effect of his fame. Tell us what he said, they beg her, their eyes shining. Tell us the exact words. But there is another aspect to the fame. Those who are in thrall to it know he will not be with them very long and this gives him the aura of someone dangerous and beautiful. He is famous, but not in the way a rabbi or a king is famous. In his presence people want to leave their lives. They want to die. They want to fall into dust and start over again. They want to give up their possessions and their families and follow him with nothing but the clothes on their back. In his presence the wealthy wonder if their wealth means anything, and the poor feel exalted for the first time in their lives. Sinners are exalted. This is why she wants to see him again, to look closely and learn something. What would she give up to follow him? If she gives up everything, would she be exalted too?

So when she hears in the marketplace that he will be at the house of Simon the leper, she resolves to go. The market idlers talk about him as if he were already dead. There have been rumours that he was to be arrested that afternoon but earned a reprieve because of the Passover, which is in two days. He is a popular man and the chief priests are afraid there will be an uprising if he is taken during the feast. When she hears this, a thought comes to her. This must be the first time unleavened bread has saved a man's life.

She stops near the city gates to see a merchant whose wares are of the highest quality. The merchant welcomes her without ceremony. He is gigantic, a bald man whose bushy beard is dyed orange. He has applied kohl around his eyes but the lines are smeared. When he calls for wine she notices that his front teeth are missing. She wonders how he eats, and she thinks she understands why he smiles so rarely. She tells him she is looking for something precious, but she doesn't know what manner of thing. The merchant nods and looks around the crowded interior of his shop as if he has never seen it before, the silk hangings and jewelled scabbards, the casks big enough for a man to hide in, the ornate drinking cups, the heavy capes and animal hides oiled to a shine. In the middle of the room is a rectangular table clear of objects. He traces the wood grain with a scarred thumb and takes his time to speak. His great stomach strains against the material of his robe. Ivory, he suggests finally, placing a tusk on the table. Or fine white linen, he says, placing a bolt of creamy fabric beside the tusk. Or both? When he grins he exposes giant yellow canines. It takes her only a moment to shake her head. He says, white wool. He says, honey and pistachio nuts, and look, I'll throw in this rare balm of Gilead. A ball of wool and a tiny bottle appear on the table. She shakes her head each time and sips at the wine. A pair of domestic slaves, says the merchant as he crosses his arms.

Strapping Israelites, who will bring honour to your house and status. A pair of peacocks – one boy, one girl? No, she says. She wants a gift that will disappear in a matter of hours and leave only a memory of pleasure. She wants to give it to a man who does not have long in the world. Peacocks and slaves mean nothing to him. He will not accept money but perhaps she can give him something more valuable, something as fleeting as he.

The merchant goes to the back of the shop into a corner lined with rugs. She hears him plundering the shelves. He is gone for a long time. She takes another mouthful of wine, which puts a fist of acid in her chest. She calms her breathing and examines her nails. She plumps up her hair and arranges it on her shoulders. The merchant returns with three flasks. He puts a drop from each on a piece of cloth and says, myrrh, frankincense, ointment of spikenard. The first two scents are familiar but the last is not. She holds it to her nostrils and inhales. A smell both strange and intimate. Human in origin. Or animal, like the sweat of an uncommon animal.

'Yes. But not in a flask. I want it in something beautiful.'

The merchant pulls aside a curtain and goes into a small space she hasn't noticed. He massages his shaped beard. He examines a case packed with vials and carved wooden casks, then selects an alabaster box. The lid is streaked with veins of scarlet. When he transfers the ointment of spikenard with a small ladle, the intimate smell is everywhere. She imagines it settling into her hair and pores. The merchant seals the box with wax and solemnly presents it to her. She feels the weight of it in her hand, soft somehow, not as heavy as marble. Even in the gloom the alabaster soaks up the light.

Leaving the merchant's shop she asks directions only once, from an old woman selling pigeons by the side of the road. Simon the leper, she says, do you know where his house is? The woman tells her where to go and adds that he isn't a leper any more. He's been cured. He now calls himself Simon the Pharisee. There is a group of men outside the house, idlers who stand around doing nothing. Where are they from? Why are there so many of them? She pushes past, the alabaster box hidden in her robe.

Inside, she finds him sitting at table with the others, some who call themselves his disciples, some who call themselves friends but are really no more than hangers-on, hanging on to his fame. There are numerous others. Silent men who watch everything, thieves and spies most likely, looking to enrich themselves in some way. The men all look alike, dark and unwashed, working men with scarred hands and cut beards. She knows him immediately. She remembers him from the times he has come to her house, first when she sat at his feet and then when he came to see them after the death and burial of her brother. And she is agape to see that her brother is there too. Lazarus is seated at the head of the table, distracted and passive, full of the heavy sighs he brought with him back from the grave. The men stare at her brother as if he is some kind of prey, a rare animal they have domesticated.

Oblivious in his cups, face purple from the wine, Lazarus sees her without seeing her. His eyes are unfocused. There is no indication that he recognises her or knows her as his beloved sister, once his favourite. He throws the wine down his gullet and immediately refills the cup, because that is the important thing, to keep the wine within reach, to keep the thoughts at bay, to feel the warmth of the liquor as it travels into the belly past the hollow fickle chest and the trickery of ribs and the heart that is nothing but obstruction. But he waits too long before the next sip and the dead thoughts return. He died and came back to life and it is the moments in between that trouble him. While dead, he discovered that the heart and the liver were interchangeable and useless, as were the kidneys, the intestines, the blood, bones and skin. There was only mind, which remained alert through the disintegration of the flesh. The mind does not die but waits, aware of the body's end and the worms that burrow into it. He knows to his great fright that this is the true experience of being dead. Consciousness of terror. There is no obliteration. The dead are awake. He reaches for the jug and fills his cup and drinks as if his thirst will never be quenched.

Her brother's expression is vacant of all emotion except boredom. She might be a stranger. There is more recognition in the way the Christ greets her. Though he is always serious, even when he makes a joke, his eyes at least are kind. To look into her brother's face is to understand that death is a kind of stupidity. His eyes are the eyes of a chicken, ferocious and empty. She will ignore him. She will not be distracted from her task. Taking a deep breath she breaks the alabaster box and pours the spikenard very slowly on the Christ's head. She saves some for his feet. For some reason she weeps a little. The tears mix with the ointment. In her confusion she dries his feet with her abundant hair and immediately the naysayers are around her, clamouring.

'But this is spikenard, used only for the anointing of the priests,' says one of the men. 'It could have been sold at market and the money used to feed the poor.'

This man has a strange way of speaking. A burst of words followed by a pause and then another burst, as if he can barely control himself. His arms are ranged on either side of his plate. He is protecting his food. It is the money she has spent on the spikenard, she thinks, noting the hungry way he looks at her. He would rob her if could.

'Why did you come here?' says the master of the house, Simon, whose face does not look diseased to her.

'Expensive and wasteful,' says the first man, the angry one. 'Are we no longer mindful of waste? What of the poor among us? What will they say who hear of such extravagance?'

It seems to her that the Christ allows the men to spend their indignation before he speaks, and when he speaks it is meant for her.

'Why do you trouble her?' he tells them. 'Let her be. As long as there is greed and cruelty the poor will always be with you. You may feed them or do them good in any way you wish, whenever you wish. I will not be with you always, or even tomorrow.'

There is a murmur among the disciples, the eager-to-please gang of idlers. No, they say. He will be there tomorrow. If he is not there, what will become of them?

'She has chosen correctly,' he says, as he said once to Martha. 'She has anointed me for the burial. Wherever this story is told, this too shall be remembered.' Then he asks her to speak her name. 'Remember,' he tells the men around the table. They are all men. She is the only woman among them. 'Remember that on the day before my death she brought a gift to sweeten my last hours.'

59

One day, these men and others like them will write their versions of the story. But when they tell the story of the woman with the ointment of spikenard they will say only that she brought with her an alabaster box, which was broken and the contents poured on Jesus's head.

In most of these accounts the woman's name is unspoken.

Some will mention that as the fragrance of the perfume filled the house, the woman washed his feet and dried them with her hair, her abundant wiry hair. They will say this was an act of wantonness. Some of the accounts will forget to mention that Jesus defended her. Others will say that one of the disciples was filled with jealousy and it was this disciple who suggested that the ointment was a waste of money, its perfume fleeting, that the poor should have been fed instead, that it was a crime against the Messiah to be the instrument of such a sin. Some sources will add the name of the disciple, Judas.

He will be named and allowed to take his place in the story.

But one name is left out of these accounts. When the gospels are written and the stories told, by men, the name of the woman is not spoken. The names of the women are not spoken, or spoken too rarely. Most often they are forgotten or suppressed or erased.

This is her name:

Mary of Bethany, sister of Martha and Lazarus.

# 8

She can do what she wants with the day. Her husband is
dead and her son has gone away for work, perhaps as far
away as Smyrna. When her husband died she did what new
widows do. She wailed. She stopped eating. She beat her
breast. Then the anguish gave way to rage and she asked
the foolish questions widows ask. Why me? Why must I
learn to be lonely? Who will take care of me now? Who
will take care of my son? But her son became a young man
with his own thoughts and his own life. The years passed.
She learned that solitude was a blessing not offered to
everyone. Her husband's death had seemed like the worst
thing that could happen to her, but in time it came to seem
like a gift tempered with bitterness. Though the memory
of his face had faded, sometimes at night she heard his voice
making a hundred complaints. Then this too faded. She is
a poor woman, as she always has been, but now she enjoys
a measure of freedom. A small measure, as much as a widow
woman is worth. There is no one to look after her, but also
there is no one to question her, or beat her, or accuse her
of idleness as her husband liked to do. She can do as she
pleases. When she hears that the man they call the Christ

is on his way to the city she decides to go to the east gate of the Temple Mount and wait. She wants to see what the famous healer looks like.

Many years later, when she is an old woman still living in the house her husband built, suffering from the usual aches and pains as well as a mysterious rash that comes and goes, she will hear people talk about the triumph of his entrance into Jerusalem. The talk will grow with the passage of time, and she will try to correct them. There was nothing triumphal about it – not for him, she will say. He was a stranger at his own feast. The clownish or demented or desperate antics of his followers. A circus he couldn't control, and the disgust was right there on his face. He tried to distance himself from the vagabonds, merchants and foreigners of all kinds that had gathered around him. But he could not. They stuck. An army of upright leeches. Many years later she will say this, but there is no one to believe her and eventually she will keep silent. Nobody cares that she was there and she remembers. They have a picture in their minds of the glory of his arrival in the city. That is the only picture in which they are interested.

That day, she is among the first to get there and she watches how the thoroughfare around the gate is transformed. The bystanders who appear from nowhere and line the road, as if waiting for a king. Vendors circulate among them, then soldiers, and the sun is directly overhead when the first travellers arrive. She sees them come down from the Mount of Olives like a troupe of entertainers. They make a noise such as she has never heard. Some are beating on hand-drums and finger-bells. Others shake rattles. There are painted donkeys and marked colts and goats. She notices a man with a horn in each hand, a trumpet and some kind of flute. When he blows on the trumpet it makes a high sound that hurts her ears. It is always the same note, always piercing. Then he plays a short melody on the flute to soothe the tempers he has roused with the trumpet. He is not a musician, none of them are, just a ragtag bunch of layabouts, including every madman who saw them passing on the road. And there are others. Charlatans and mountebanks who boast of cures for her ailments. Men leading livestock they wish to sell, or touting raw honey and withered figs and used slaves for the market. Young men and women singing or laughing for no reason she can imagine, their laughter as shrill as the trumpet.

At first it makes her afraid. Has the whole world gone mad? What are they so happy about? But then she sees the man they call the Christ, surrounded on all sides by revellers, and she sees that he is the only one among them who is not singing, who is not laughing, whose face falls when he catches sight of the city gates. To her astonishment he hangs his head and weeps, while all around him the rabble continues to dance, making up jokes and foolish games, lost to reason. It is the sight of a stricken man in the midst of carelessness that makes her want to follow him and discover the reason for his tears.

The crowd senses the change in his mood as he enters the gates of the city. The men stop their songs of ribaldry. The women stop dancing. The hosannas begin. But the drums continue to beat and at intervals the man with the trumpet blows his single dissonant note. She sees that some of the men, possibly drunk, are breaking small branches from the trees to smooth the dust on the road. One of them takes off his cloak with a flourish and spreads it on the ground for the uncaring crowd to walk on. Years later, when some of the day's events are unclear in her memory, she will recall the man's face, the colour of his beard, the fact that his cloak was of fine wool, the look of satisfaction when he spread it on the muddy road and invited her to step upon it, and when she did, how tiny her steps became, how wayward, the steps of a cat, or a young unmarried woman yet to bear a child, yet to be abandoned, yet to fend for herself.

She follows at the edge of the shambling dusty group. When they come within sight of the temple the Christ dismounts from his donkey. His bones are sore from the long hours of riding. Someone calls for silence. But there are too many of them and silence is not possible. She notices that the Christ has changed. He seems no longer sad but angry, the emotion she knows best. Her husband was a master of it. He tells the crowd that he and some of his followers will go to Bethany for the night. They will be back in the morning and they will enter the temple.

'Do you think you have the right to be happy?' he asks.

Confused voices say yes, yes.

'You are chosen, you are blessed, you have done the good deeds.'

Yes, say the voices, yes, oh lord, yes.

'You have stayed away from sin and rebuked the sinners. Is that what you think?'

'No,' a woman says, 'I don't.'

'You do. All of you do. You think God the Father has chosen you as his vessels of happiness. Isn't that right?'

He drops his voice to a whisper. She tries to go closer to hear but the crowd is too thick. The smell of sweat and stale wine is too heavy for her. When she is finally close enough she hears only a few words:

'Jerusalem, your house is forsaken. You kill your children and stop up the throats of your prophets.'

The words are taken up as a chant. Someone makes a song of it and they all join in.

*O Jerusalem, Jerusalem, your house is new forsaken,*
*Jerusalem, Jerusalem, your prophets all are broken.*

It is dark and the lamplighters begin to light the torches. As if darkness is a signal, the crowd turns rowdy again. The song picks up volume, some of the better singers adding boastful touches. A barrel by the entrance is overturned. Abandoned sandals are strewn across the road. The crowd surges against the walls. The priests take fright and lock the doors of the temple. For a moment it seems as if the mob will force its way in. There are shouts for justice and wine. But when the Christ and his followers leave, the shouts dissipate into half-hearted calls for revolution. Some of the revellers fall asleep where they are standing, curled up on the road like sufferers felled by a new plague.

Picking her way carefully among the standing or fallen bodies, she walks home. Her feet ache and her head feels heavy. On her street the pole-raised lamp has stopped burning. The sky is purple, the air still. She lets her legs carry her into the front courtyard, where she washes her feet before entering the house. Inside she lights the lamp and walks from the front room to the back, unseeing, oblivious to the space she has lived in for most of her life. Her head is full of words and echoes. The shouts of the crowd are in her ears. The wild hosannas and awful laughter. She makes a small meal, a handful of dried dates with unleavened bread and oil. She takes fresh water from the well. Then she feeds the goats and the hens and collects the eggs to sell at the market in the morning. As she falls asleep the question comes back to her. Why did he cry at the sight of Jerusalem? Did he see every last sorrow the city would endure in the next few days and in the hundreds and thousands of years to come? Or was there another reason?

She wakes late and dresses hurriedly and puts some dried fruit in a twist of sackcloth. On her walk to the temple she passes the market and realises she has forgotten to bring the milk and eggs. It is the first morning in all these years that she has neglected her duties. But she won't turn back. There is bad luck in turning back once you have set out on a journey. She quickens her pace as she passes the houses of the Pharisees, a route she has taken a hundred times, today somehow unfamiliar, and as she turns the corner into the main road to the temple the answer comes to her. He cried because he beheld his own future. He looked at Jerusalem and saw the true vision of his death. He was not crying for the city or its inhabitants. He was crying for himself.

The sun is already bright and her cloak heavy on her shoulders, her feet still aching from the day before. The heat makes her light-headed but the dizziness passes. The noise is unbearable as she nears the temple. The revellers are back, unwashed and bleary-eyed, already drunk though it is early in the day. She notices that they are no longer laughing and she feels it again, the nearness of violence, how easily it might erupt.

She looks for the man they call the Christ and finds him in the centre of the same group of men who went with him to Bethany. She wonders at how placid they are, his chosen companions, who seem barely conscious of what is happening around them, much less that they are in the midst of something momentous. They speak only among themselves. When someone in the crowd steps forward to give them something, food or drink or some other kind of gift, they accept without enthusiasm. As if it is their right to receive bounty from the people. They never say thank you. At times they don't even look up or acknowledge the person who stands before them. They are distracted and she understands they are waiting for something. They want the crowd at its thickest. They hope to be protected by the others.

Someone begins to sing the song from the day before. New verses have been added during the night:

*O Jerusalem, Jerusalem, broken are your children's bones.*
*Jerusalem, Jerusalem, broken on your cruel stones.*

Some join in but not the Christ or the men who surround him. Soon the voices die down into the surrounding chaos. When the crowd has swollen so much that no man can walk through, he pushes his way into the temple. The fervour that has built for two days and a night finds its release at last in the sound of splintering. This is the signal for which the drunken and the furious have been waiting. They pick up the tables at which the moneylenders sit and throw them into the street. Some of the moneylenders are thrown out too, faces bloodied and their clothes ruined. She watches as men fight their way through the crowd to land a blow on a particular man, someone to whom they owe money. Scores are settled and new ones tallied. Someone picks up a wooden dove cage and smashes it against the wall of the temple. A flock of frightened birds is released into the crowd. A water bearer is beaten, the water spilled about his feet. One of the twelve says to the confused bearer that no vessels will be allowed into the temple. At last she hears the voice. *Is it not written that my house shall be called of all nations the house of prayer?* The moneylenders to whom he poses this question are too frightened to reply. They are trying to placate the mob. The voice rings out again. *You have made it a den for thieves to buy and sell.*

When the moneylenders and merchants have fled and his followers are comfortable in the halls of the temple, he calls the crowd to order. He speaks of his journey to Jerusalem, days of riding on a donkey across the highlands of the north, he and his small group of men, their backs aching and their bones weary with travel. He knew there were ancient trees on the hills they traversed, but many of them had been cut down to build the houses in the towns they passed, and the towns they passed did not seem to him like the work of men. They were not dwellings built by human hands. No, they seemed instead to be as ancient as the hills, as implacable as the sun or a storm at sea, as green as the river banks of Egypt that he had seen as a child, and as patient and unmoving as the crocodiles on the banks of the river. Then he tells stories she cannot understand. He speaks in pictures and riddles. He speaks of fig trees that cannot bear fruit, of mountains cast into the sea by the power of faith and seas become dry land by the power of the will, of words with the power to make prophecies come true, of the necessity for forgiveness, and he ends with yet another question. If men do not forgive each other, then how will they be forgiven by God?

She is taken by the truth of this assertion. Her anger against her husband (for dying without warning) and her son (for disappearing) had long ago hardened into spite that she has turned against herself, aided by bitterness and solitude. She understands it now because of this man's question about forgiveness, and she thinks it may happen soon, the wall inside her may melt at last. She wants to speak to him.

As she makes her way through the crowd she passes a group that has taken refuge under a temple awning. She hears the words 'punishment' and 'penalty'. She hears their anger against those who are taken in by a man who calls himself the Son of God and wishes to destroy the property of the temple. He will visit violence upon the men who embody its true authority. He is an agent of foreign powers. She hears the last phrase clearly and she wants to warn him.

She finds him sitting against a wall. The rowdies have spread their cloaks over flattened bales of hay. Some have taken up a collection. A steady stream of people enters the outer courtyard to throw money on a blanket someone has spread on the ground. The rich scatter handfuls of silver, denarii that they treat carelessly, bidding to buy salvation or hoping for protection from the wrath of the multitude.

She opens the money purse hanging on her belt and takes out two copper mites, which she places hesitantly on a corner of the blanket. When she looks up, he is watching her. He is looking at the old cloak she made herself and repaired over the years, each tear proclaiming her status of widowed wife and abandoned mother.

Look, he says, look at the widow who has given more with her two mites than all the others who cast into the treasury. For they have cast of their abundance and she, in her want, cast all she had.

The poor widow's generosity has been mentioned in the gospels. But her name has been lost and here is returned:

Junia, widow of Jerusalem.

# 9

Write this down, Mary, write that the dream always ends
the same way. I return to the hill with the name of my
death, Golgotha, the name I saw in the dreams of my death
before I dreamed it on the hill. And though it turned and
returned I remember the first time I dreamed it, and again
as I entered the gates of Jerusalem, knowing it would be
the last time, and the cruelty of the city made me weep. I
knew what the future would bring. Nearby to the cruel
city I saw it in the faces of the multitude, in the faces of
the children, in the eyes of the sheep and the cries of the
hawk. I saw it in the garden of the oil press on the night
I willed them to take me, the night of the doubt and the
release. I saw it at dawn on the waves of the lake of
Capernaum. I saw it countless times when I was alone in
the desert and the terrible visions were upon me. But I saw
it first as a child when I saw the story of my death on the
face of the woman who sat on the road to Israel eating her
meal, and we stopped at the inn by the wayside and I saw
her. I could not eat my own loaf. I tried but could not eat.
For all this I declared that the innocent, the poor and the
lowly and the works they create are safe in the hands of

God, for God *is* the innocent and the guilty. That no man knows to live or not live by looking at what is before him. I went to the eating woman and spoke the words that troubled me. I said, what ails you that it shows on your face though you shed no tears? I asked why the food she ate brought her no pleasure and the finery she wore she would give to a beggar and nothing she saw or said or heard, nothing she might think or dream would bring her joy. But she did not reply. Or she replied by looking at the men who sat with her, as if taking their permission to speak, and then she looked at me as if to tell me she had not their permission. I spoke to her as a parent, not a child. I said the same food comes to the sinner and to the saint, to the wise man in his tower and to the fool in the dust, to the good and to the wicked, to the harlot and to the priest, to the thief in the dock and to the judge on high – the same meal at the end. It is in the yearning that difference is made.

# 10

After her brother's death, people come to know her name, and her sister's name, and the name of her poor brother. When he is no longer the sweet boy she has known and no longer answers to the name he has carried all his life. The Christ's visit brings more than just the fame that accompanies fame. With the raising of her brother from the dead her family comes to the attention of the powerful and the cruel. Those men who would crush them as they would ants on an anthill, elders who wish him dead a second time but truly killed, because his story makes Jews wish to leave the synagogue and join Christ. Yet what could they have done differently?

That morning, on a day that begins like any other day, she readies the meal with her sister. They call for Lazarus when the table is set, but he is always slow in the morning. When he does not appear they pay it no mind.

Mary says, 'Do you remember the stories Imma used to tell us when we were very small?'

'I don't,' she replies.

'Don't you remember the story of David and his many wives?'

'She never told you that story. I told you.'

'No, it was Imma. She told us that David and his six hundred men demanded money from Abigail's husband. Or else they would rob him or murder him.'

'Nabal. The husband's name was Nabal and he refused to pay protection money.'

'See, now you remember.'

'Of course I remember, I'm the one told you the story!' And she tells it again.

When David was a young killer and thief he had to hide in the mountains to escape his murderous father-in-law, Saul. In time he became the leader of a prosperous gang of criminals. Once, at shearing season, he asked a rich old man for money in exchange for not killing him. The old man refused. He insulted David's ancestors, his future progeny and his worthiness in the eyes of God. David and four hundred of his men put on their swords and thought to visit the man. They would convince him. One way or another they would make him pay. Not far from old Nabal's house they came across his young wife, Abigail, who had loaded up two donkeys with choice foods and wine. Do not attack my husband and my home, she begged David. Do you see the gifts I bring you? A lifelong womaniser, David was inflamed by the beauty of Nabal's wife. He agreed. Abigail went home to tell her husband that she had saved the household from the wrath of four hundred armed men. But Nabal was at a feast, drinking himself unconscious, a long process that would continue until the second watch of the night. She waited until morning and then she roused him from his sleep to tell him what she had done. They say old Nabal's face instantly turned purple. Before he could say a word against his wife, he fell off the bed clutching his chest. In ten days he was dead. Was it fear at the disaster that had almost occurred or anger at his wife that killed him? Abigail had no time to think too deeply on the answer. When David heard the old man was dead and his widow had inherited his riches, he wasted no time in making her his wife.

'What a woman she was,' says Mary to her sister. 'Whenever I think of her, I think of you. You are that kind of woman. You will do what needs be done. You won't hesitate.'

Who would consider this a compliment? Abigail may have been strong-willed but how much is strength of will worth in relation to loyalty? She betrayed her old husband for a younger one, who betrayed her and became king, and never stopped his lustful ways, coveting the wives of other men, sending his rivals to their deaths, threatening or cheating whoever stood in his way, a rapist who let the rape of his own daughter go unavenged so as to safeguard his firstborn son. What honour was there in being the wife of such a man? But she does not say this to Mary. Instead she tells her sister that it is another of David's wives she should bless with her regard, Michal, the daughter of Saul.

'Do you remember what her father asked for a bride price?' she asks.

Mary says she does not remember.

'A hundred Philistine foreskins,' she says. 'But David gave him two hundred, a double dowry. That is how much he wanted Michal.'

She tries to imagine David, the criminal king surrounded by his four hundred criminal followers, counting foreskins with their quick blunt fingers. It was said there were all shapes and sizes, including the foreskins of children snatched from their mothers and those of old men killed in their beds. Two hundred foreskins! How did they carry them around? In a bag, or a large fisherman's basket? Did they kill two hundred men and boys or did they circumcise them and let them live, this being David's way of showing Saul his value both as a son-in-law and a protector of the faith?

'He didn't care about Michal,' Mary says quietly. 'He would do anything to be king.'

'It doesn't matter,' she says, 'he did what he was good at and he continued doing it, day after day, year after year. He developed a taste for it when he killed the lumbering old giant who was too sick to fight. It was all he knew to do, to kill efficiently. As time passed he expanded his scope, sacked entire cities, murdered Philistines and Edomites, Moabites and Ammonites. And so he became our most beloved killer king.'

She thinks: what if she and Mary had been born as boys? How different their lives would have been. They might have been kings too, but wise ones, who would not shed the blood of thousands just to sit on a throne.

She calls, louder now, for her brother to come to breakfast.

But her brother does not rise from his bed. And when they enter his room they find him shaking with fever. His skin is so hot nothing will cool him. They send for the family healer, who says her brother is a danger to them. He should be tied to the bed. Over the next few days the fever gets worse. When they call to him, his eyes come open and he stares, though he says nothing. On his face they see no glimmer of recognition. He cries out in a language they cannot understand, hoarse cries in a voice they have never heard. At night he shakes, screaming in terror, but his sisters refuse to tie him down. He says a lion-headed female demon is in the room. Lamashtu, he cries, Lamashtu is here, stop her, why can't you stop her? But how can they stop someone they cannot see? Lamashtu advances upon their house and cannot be deterred. On the way she steals babies who suckle on their mothers, entering the wombs of pregnant women, hovering above Lazarus, cooing delightedly that he must feed at her dugs.

The next morning she hears that the Christ is on the road, not far from Bethany. She sends word. Please come, Lazarus is sick. But the messenger returns with strange news. The Christ has made camp and will not move. He is resting, or waiting.

'Waiting for what?'

'He didn't say.'

'But what reason did he give?'

'He did not give a reason,' the messenger says, 'and there was no sign that he heard me, or cared to listen.'

But he must have heard. She hears he is nearby with a troupe of travelling entertainers who claim to be his followers. By then her brother has been dead four days, dead and buried, and she has been waiting for six, watching the road for signs of the Christ. Instead of coming directly to the house he has stopped at an old well on the road. When she hears this she goes to him, while her sister prefers to stay in her room, as she has done since her brother's death. It strikes her that Mary has sunk into mourning as into a soft bed. She is comfortable with silence and tears. It is as if she enjoys grief, has nurtured and befriended it in the hope that it might grow. But she is not like her sister. She has always been the bold one, the older one who protected her. And because she is older she is loved less. Her brother and sister are loved more. This too is the way it has always been. She is older. She will not wallow. She will brook no shyness in the way she works upon the earth. When she finds the Christ in the midst of the entertainers and pickpockets and storytellers that surround him, she says:

'Why do you keep company with those who are unworthy of you?'

She tells him they have been waiting so many days she has lost count. He could have saved her brother from his terrible death of trembling and ague. And though Lazarus, whom he loved, is dead now four days, death cannot be the end. For he is the Son of God and he has appeared amongst them to remind them that there is beauty on the earth and a purpose to their lives. That behind everything, little or great, wondrous or common, there is the sifting hand. He is the son, and whatever he asks of his father, his father will provide. Please, she says, her voice breaking at last. Bring him back, my brother whom you loved as your own. The Christ says only:

'The brother is not dead. He lives.'

'He does not live, she replies. I know his life as I know my own. Didn't I breathe on his lips to bring him back? Didn't I see how cold he had become, how far he had moved from us? But if you so will it, he will rise even now, at this moment. The crowd has grown. They are there to witness a miracle. The great story being written, in which each spectator has a part, however small. She thinks it possible that he is reluctant to perform for a crowd of rowdies and drunks. Why else would he hesitate?

This is when she has the idea. She goes home and brings Mary to him. Her quiet, clever sister who says nothing. She only kneels at his feet and weeps, and yet the tears have more effect than all of her own words. It has always been this way, from when they were little. All Mary has to do is weep and she gets whatever she wants. And now, as she holds the hem of his tunic, the Christ too is weeping, he is so touched by her sister's tears.

(This is the story of the women who weep.)

All her entreaties are as nothing in the face of Mary's sobs. The beseeching shape her eyebrows take. Her soft manner and childlike voice. She falls to her knees and lifts the hem of his tunic and kisses it and says nothing, not a single word, and yet he is transformed into a man of action. Urgency returns and he gets to his feet at last. At last he goes to the graveside and gives the command for her brother to rise. But her brother does not rise. There is not a stirring, not a breath that disturbs the soil of the grave. She imagines the dead in their thousands under her feet, hands reaching up towards the light, and the thousands under them, layer upon layer of the dead. What if they all were to rise? How would she find her poor brother? When he gives a second command, her brother is pulled from the grave as if by strong hands. Earth clings to his hair, a dirty kitchen rag on his face, the winding cloths loose and his nails caked with filth. There are cries of dismay from the watchers. Mary reaches for him. He staggers towards his sisters and stops, his expression blank. In the stumble of his feet: the remnant of a memory his body will not relinquish. Unconscious, he recognises no one. Not his sisters, not the relatives who have gathered at the house to mourn him, not the friends and traders who have come to pay their last respects. He is loved. He has always been loved. Yet now he seems bewildered by those who love him, and by the heart that beats in his ribs, and by the blood that has begun to move in his veins. He is overcome by listlessness and also by fear, who was always bright and fearless.

The terrible thought comes to her then, to ask the Christ if it was not better to take back his gift. He has interfered with the natural order of time. The man who returned is not her brother, only a copy of him. His ghost has returned to the world and he stayed in the grave. But she keeps the thought to herself. How can she say such a thing? She and her sister have begged him to bring back their brother. He has done so reluctantly and her brother has returned reluctantly. They must accept the gift they have been given, however bitter it is in the tasting. It is not easy to love her brother in his new state. Where he was beautiful he is gross, and where he was lively he is dull. The boy who knew how to charm even the wicked, how to say exactly the thing that would make the meanest man or woman love him, that boy is gone. In his place is a bewildered man who takes nothing seriously except his one task. To drink as much as he can from the moment he wakes to the moment he falls unconscious on his bed, or on the street, or in some low tavern.

He eats all day and he drinks. As the weeks and months pass, the shape of his face changes. His hair thins and there is a smell from him of loam and snails. A scent she comes in time to identify as that of the grave. He leaves it on his clothes, on the table and chairs, on the utensils they eat with. She smells it in the air. He has become so fat that his clothes must be let out. His manner changes. He speaks little, without affection. He tries to avoid being in the same room as his sisters. When he does speak it is to demand food and wine, or money, in a harsh tone as if they are his servants. Some nights he does not come home. On those nights, though they will never admit it to each other, they are happy to be without him.

Then there is the company he keeps. The strange men who adhere to him from the taverns in which he has drunk. They come to the house at odd hours and look too familiarly at Mary. One night she sees a man standing at the end of the road. The pole-raised lamplight is weak and she is unable to make out his features. Is he drunk or spying? What is he spying on? Then she notices the men in the market, on the roads of the city, on the road to Jerusalem. She notices them in the temple. Men she has never seen before, who somehow appear when her brother is there. She is frightened by the way they look at him. As if they are weighing his flesh by the shekel and the talent, to judge how much his meat will fetch in the market. She understands what they see when they look at him. They see him dead. They want him dead again. It is their only wish.

Early one morning she finds a body slumped against the gate. Her brother, alive, with a fresh wound on the back of his head. She brings him in and tends to him, cleaning the wound as well as she can. She and Mary put him to bed, where he falls noisily asleep. They consider their young brother, the boy they loved and protected. No trace of that boy remains.

In the afternoon he wakes and roars for wine. When it is brought he drinks deeply and holds the bowl up for more. He has no explanation for the wound on his head. He will not tell them where he was the night before. He only demands more wine and drinks deeply and continues to drink until his head falls against the bedpost and the house subsides into blessed silence. Mary comes to her then, to hold her sister as she weeps. For the first time since her childhood she too gives in to tears. She cries for the years in which she had to be the strong one, the older one, the one who sacrificed her tears for the sake of her brother and sister.

This is the story of the women who weep and this is the story of Martha of Bethany, sister of Mary and Lazarus.

# 11

David was a lustful and murderous king who was admired by the faithful. Once, at the temple in Galilee, someone pointed out the Christ. Someone else said, but how can the Christ come out of Galilee? Didn't the scriptures say he will be of the seed of David and will come out of Bethlehem, where David was? Still others, Pharisees and rulers among them, thought to arrest him. They wished to flay his skin from the flesh, for sport. They said, no prophet will arise out of Galilee. They said, the man is false and his claims are blasphemy. But no one laid a hand on him. Each went to his own home, except the Christ, who had no home and spent the night in the open on the Mount of Olives.

As he sleeps, a woman is awake on the upper floor of a house in Galilee. She is unused to the softness of the bed. The frame is made of solid wood, which feels strange to her compared to the packed earth under the bed in her home. The blanket is made of wool, not goat's hair. It smells different. The feel of it against her skin is too smooth to be comfortable. She wants her own bed and her husband beside her on the mattress they share, in the room divided by a sheet to separate their sleeping area from the space where the animals sleep.

The woman describes herself as a Sumerian when she is asked, and in Galilee she is asked, often, whether she is a Hittite or a Canaanite. They ask if everyone is dark where she is from, and if she was taken as a slave. She tells them she is no slave. Some people are dark and others fair. It makes no difference in the country where she was born. She never says she is a Canaanite. Her future husband came to her country as a foreigner. He lived in their midst and became prosperous. He caught sight of her once as he passed their house and thought to take her for his wife. When he went to her father with a proposal of marriage he was told to come back the next day. Her father explained to her that the man who wished to be her husband was of Israel, and the God of Israel had commanded the extermination of all Canaanites, women, girls, infants, men, the peaceful and the warlike, the wicked and the just, and the vast numbers of those in between.

'Israel's God,' said her father, 'has forbidden intermarriage with the daughters of Israel. If he takes you to Israel, you will be for ever an outsider.'

A year after the marriage her husband decided to return to his home in Galilee. She followed him because he had paid a bride price for her. He was her husband and it was her duty to go with him, however poor they would be in Israel. If you say we will be poor, we will be poor, her husband told her. He called her Huldah, after a woman he heard about in the old days in Jerusalem who told the fates of nations and kings. They said Huldah had the gift of prophecy. Her husband gave her the name because he was convinced she had a black tongue and what she said would come to pass.

'What does "Huldah" mean?' she asked him once.

'Weasel,' her husband replied with a rare smile. 'No, wrong word, more like a mole.'

'How am I like a mole?' she asked.

'You can stay in bed under the covers for longer than anyone in the world,' her husband said. 'You are a prophet and a mole.'

He has called her Huldah for so long she sometimes forgets the name she was born with, Ariamma. She was thirteen summers when he bought her from her parents. She is middle-aged now, which means she has been Huldah longer than she was Ariamma. She likes being Huldah. It makes her feel as powerful and wise as the woman she was named after, even if she is neither of those things. Or she would cure her husband who has been sick for more than a year. He took to his bed when the palsy froze his left side into an expression of misery. It was as if someone had taken a rod and drawn it down the middle of his face and continued all the way to his belly. His right side was normal but the left drooped, and the droop became permanent. He needed to be looked after and she should be with him now. She has left food and water by his bedside, but sometimes from frustration he refuses to eat. She wants to go home. And first she wants to be paid.

What else could she have done, other than the thing that brought her to this strange bed that is so comfortable she

85

cannot sleep? They would have starved. There is goat's milk that she makes into cheese and cooks with lemons. Sometimes there is bread. But there are days when there is no bread or milk. When she told him, he wept with the shame. She did not. There was no other way, she said, and he knew it as the truth. And so the day before she went to the city gates in the evening at a time no respectable man or woman would be there. She adjusted her veil and wrapped her cloak tight. Soon a man stopped to talk. He was old, which she liked. She noticed the rings on his fingers and the rich material of his robe.

'Why are you here?' he asked, looking full in her eyes.

'Why do you want me to be here?' she said, noting a small scar on the bridge of his nose and the fine net of wrinkles around his mouth.

He said, 'Are you waiting for someone?'

'I was waiting, I'm not any more.'

That was all it took. He led her to a house not far from her own home, and she wondered how many of the men who saw her on the way recognised her. With the veil drawn across her face, only her eyes could be seen, but that was enough. Her eyes were her distinctive feature.

The old man is snoring beside her now, as first light seeps into the room. When should she ask for the money? Or will he offer it to her before she leaves? She prays he will. Should she have fixed the amount before they came here? Perhaps, but this is her first time. She is not practised at whoredom. She is a poor woman with a husband to protect. The old man had not been gentle. But he had climbed on top of her and lifted his tunic and finished quickly. At least he had been quick. He had not bothered undressing her. He had tried to kiss her and afterwards he looked miserable, as if he might burst out wailing. He'd gone to the far side of the bed, careful not to touch her. She had wanted to ask him something then. If you feel bad about what we did, how do you think I feel?

Her husband will not be asleep. He is awake, she knows. He is worried about her and sleepless, as always. She cannot stay still. She sits up on the wooden bed that creaks at the slightest movement. It is dawn. If she leaves now, there is less chance she will be seen by the neighbours. She will wake up the old man, accept the money she has earned and she will go home. And that is when she hears a noise on the street, followed by shouts and the sound of heavy feet on the stairs.

Afterwards she tries to remember the order in which it happened but she cannot. Was she on her feet when they came in? The old man, was he on his feet or lying down? She isn't sure. What she remembers is the shouting and the sudden appearance of a group of men, so many that the room fills up with the smell of sweat and unwashed hair. What she will not forget is the way they grab her and the way they threaten the old man. He threatens them too. He tells them he is an elder of the temple and he will ruin them if they dare to touch him. Two of the men take her by the arms and drag her down the stairs to the front door. She is not frightened by any of it. Not even when they pull her through the streets to the temple, and people on the way avert their eyes or stare like she is some kind of criminal. She is not wearing her veil. Her face is naked to their eyes.

'Why are you looking at me?' she shouts. 'Is it a crime to be poor?'

Some of the passers-by recoil as if she is a lunatic, and for a moment she knows what it means to be mad. You don't care how you look to others. You have no shame and no fear. You are free. At the main square the fisherwomen are setting up the catch of the morning in neat rows. They at least don't stare. Then, near a cleared field by the square, she sees a woman like her, alone, hair matted, barefoot in a dirty tunic. She is pointing to the sky and singing. *Listen to your name on the wind.* The woman smiles as she goes past, held firmly by the men. Through the streaks of dirt on her face and the matted hair, her smile reveals a full set of white teeth. She sees that the woman is young. *The wind says blood is coming and it is not yours.* And then she smiles again, as if to say, I am a woman speaking to a woman and I wish to tell you only this, we shall endure. We shall endure longer than the men.

She takes this as a message from the spirit of her namesake. The prophet Huldah is telling her there is nothing to fear. Those who have laid hands on her are without protection in the world that really matters, the one that exists beyond the surface of things. For the first time, as she looks at the faces of the men who are rushing her through the streets, the rough men who work in the fields and sleep in the open, the bearish black-bearded unwashed men, it becomes clear to her that they do not know what is in store for them. They know only that they are sharing an adventure. They are unable to conceal their excitement. Among them she sees the old man she has spent the night with. He is now part of the mob that has taken her liberty, the cruel old man who still has not paid her, who has ensured that her sacrifice has been in vain. And all at once she knows what will happen to him and the others, knows it with a certainty that dazzles her. As if she is seeing through Huldah's eyes the overturned cart that crushes, the mauling by dogs, the elder in fine clothes dead of the wasting disease, the old man she lay with stoned to death. But how can it be? Isn't she the one to die by stoning?

When they get to the temple it is late in the morning. There is a noisy crowd that has taken up position in the outer courtyard. It spills into the streets around the temple complex. There are soldiers and Pharisees and scribes, but also families, working men and women, others who look like thieves or murderers, a juggler, stray dogs, more lunatics. All of these wastrels and criminals congregate around a slender man with a cropped beard and dark skin who squats under a dead tree, an olive tree perhaps, she isn't sure. She has never learned the vegetation of the place she has lived in for so long. In her mind they are the great oak trees of her home country. The man in the centre of the group is speaking in a low voice and she cannot catch the words. He stops speaking when they approach.

One of the men who took her prisoner is an older man with a braided beard. He carries a leather truncheon and stays at the back of the group and refuses to soil his hands by touching her. He tells the slender man that she has been caught in the act of adultery. There is no doubt she is an adulteress, for she was found in the bed of someone who is not her husband. At this, she looks for the man she has stayed the night with, but they have gripped her by the neck and she cannot turn. The elder with the truncheon continues to talk and it is hard to believe the thing that he is saying with his measured manner and beard and expensive clothes. Did not the law of Moses tell us there was only one punishment for a woman like her? Only one punishment equal to her sin? We will stone her to the death. Do you not agree, he asks the man, who does not reply. He is absorbed in writing something on the ground with his finger. She wonders for a moment if he too is a lunatic, if somehow the whole world has gone lunatic at the same time. What if he is writing a message meant for her? Does he not know she cannot read? What if only she can see him writing on the ground?

They are trying to trick you. Don't say anything, somebody in the crowd says to the man.

He continues to write on the packed brown dirt. What is he writing? What could be so important that he must keep writing in his imaginary book while the people around him decide whether a woman dies or lives? There is chaos, many people shouting at once that she be put to death. People point at her and scream, Whore! A chant goes up. Stone her! The men who took her join in. Stone her! The old man who slept with her, whose foul spittle she can still taste, he is shouting too. He is hoarse from shouting. Who in the crowd would imagine that a few hours ago this old man had lain with the woman he now wishes dead?

And still the man continues to write, as if he is God writing on a tablet with his finger. A slender god adding a new commandment to confirm that she must be put to death in the ancient law.

She is not expecting it when the man says something that makes her captors disappear, the men who had begun to gather the stones and boulders of her execution. Even the shameless old man who still hasn't paid her, even he disappears at the slender man's words that are spoken so loudly they can be heard by everyone, including those in the street outside:

*Let him who is without sin cast the first stone.*

And when he sees the men are gone, who would have stoned her to death, he asks who has condemned her. He speaks clearly for one who spoke so softly before. No one, she says, no one has condemned me. Her breath leaves her body at what he says next:

*Go, and sin no more.*

She would like to be one of those who have taken up position in the courtyard of the temple. She can tell that something is about to happen and the man will be at the centre of it. But she must hurry to her husband.

She has no money and she is alive. She hears the wind in the branches of the dead tree above her. *The wind says blood is coming.* To the slender man she offers thanks. She says:

I am Ariamma the Canaanite, named Huldah by my husband.

# 12

He was always travelling in those days. From city to village to a hamlet in the desert, talking to those who would listen. This was when he still believed in talking. The twelve went with him. Twelve men for the twelve tribes. At the time they were a tight jealous circle that did not allow outsiders or women. But that was soon to change. She would be the first female disciple and leader of the travelling church. After her there would be another, and another. Women among the disciples. Though you would not know it from the accounts written later by the men.

It begins when her mother hears that the man they call Jesus is in Magdala for the night. A crowd of vagabonds follows in his wake, all kinds of foreigners and freed slaves, spies too, and vendors of miracle cures. It is more festive than the market, she says. He is healing the sick, the halt, the blind. Her mother wants Mary to see him. What if he is able to help her? But her father says the whole town will be there, everyone they know. As it is they talk about her grown brother who has the mind of a child. Why make a drama out of their small household matters? In any case she is better. Other than the weeping, she is almost normal.

Who knows, soon the weeping might stop. He goes on like this and he would have got his way, except that she comes out of her room wet-eyed and dressed, determined to go. Her father cannot stop her.

It is the first time in three weeks that she has washed her hair, the first time in a month she has put on clean clothes. She is so thin her tunic hangs from her shoulders like a rag, and the shape of her face has changed. The thought of food fills her with anguish. Mealtimes are doom-laden, the whole family waiting to see if she will put a morsel of meat into her mouth. Sometimes her mother looks at her and starts to cry and then she cries too, if she isn't crying already. She does not stop until she has exhausted herself. She cries in her sleep and wakes to wetness on the pillow. The moment she wakes she cries until her chest hurts.

They set off in the afternoon. They follow the crowd, which becomes more raucous the closer they get. She sees footwear abandoned in the middle of the road. A single sandal flipped over, then more sandals. Where have the wearers gone? Has there been a massacre? A stampede? She wants to collect the sandals in a basket and offer them to the barefoot men and women they encounter on the way. So many with the same dazed expression on their faces. How can one man have such an effect on so many? People behaving as if they have survived a catastrophe, hysterical or numb – so much shared distress she forgets her own troubles. For the first time in days she is not crying and the heaviness in her chest begins to slip free. When they get to the well near which he and his men have set up camp, the crowd is so thick her father considers turning back. How will they get past the men and women whose hysteria seems to spread by a touch or a look or a tremor of air?

Further up she sees a frail woman, old before her time, accompanied by some men. There is a space around them, as if people don't want to get too close. It is a strange sight in the midst of the tumult. An old woman who has created an area around herself that nobody will disturb. Her father tells her it is the Christ's mother and brothers, and they too are unable to get near him because of the press of wild-eyed people. Then one of his disciples comes through the throng with a message for his mother, whose name is also Mary. The messenger's manner is as cruel as his words. He will not be able to see you, he tells the old woman.

'Not see his mother?' says one of the men. 'Not see his brothers? We want to hear it from him.'

'He told me to bring you this message.'

'What message? And who are you?'

'The master's trusted friend.'

'Well, trusted friend, can't you see how exhausted his mother is? We've been waiting all day. Tell us what he said.'

'I did.'

'Tell us the exact words.'

'He said, Who is my mother? Who are my brothers?'

'This is his mother, this old woman whose heart is breaking.'

'When I told him you were waiting, he pointed to the crowd and said, They are my mothers and my brothers.'

The messenger tells the old woman he knows she will hear her son's words and understand them and do as she is commanded. But the old woman's confusion only deepens. She asks the man to repeat the message, nodding her head at the words that mean nothing. After some time she and the men retreat into the crowd. The woman limps slightly, disappointment plain on her face.

As they walk away, Mary notices that the old woman is barefoot. She is one of those who lost their sandals. She marvels at the cruelty of the Christ. The way he has separated himself from the past. The way he has given birth to himself, invented his own history and rejected his parents. She looks at her own parents standing where they are, buffeted by the crowd. As evening falls they sit on the dusty road. When it gets darker some in the crowd melt away, while others light oil lamps and lay out bedding and blankets against the night. Her father buys two coarse goat's-hair blankets from a man selling things from the back of his mule. He buys a loaf, which they eat with oil. They try to sleep. She wakes all of a sudden before dawn. When she knows she is awake the tears come, unbidden and unstoppable.

Her mother takes her hand and they make their way to the well. They step across sleeping figures, entire families huddled together for warmth. She knows him by his still-ness. He sits cross-legged in the centre of a group of sleeping men. Immediately her mother starts to speak. She tells him about Mary's affliction, the demon of sadness that has taken hold of her and filled her days with tears. He gestures for silence and addresses Mary.

'Why do you weep?' he says to her, the very words he will say many years later when everything has changed. 'Can you not see that which is in front of your eyes?'

They sit together in silence as the sky lightens and as her mother weeps, her own tears stop.

He says, 'Go, the demon has left you.'

The day's heat has begun and some of the men who travel with him are awake. In time, when these men come to write their accounts of what happened that day they will cite the seven demons that are released from her. They will write that the demons that left her were the demons of lust and sin. Hundreds of years later, men who have never met her will call her a fallen woman. A prostitute who renounced evil. She will be called a sinner, when her only sin is that she is from a prosperous home and she is sad.

That day she stays by the well after her parents have returned home, sitting as close to him as she can. By afternoon the crowd swells again. There are more people than the day before. She notices the multitude of the sick, paraded by their families as if they are creatures of fable brought from a foreign country. Men and women with every kind of ailment, visible and hidden, suppurating boils, flowering warts, mysterious bruises and wounds, men and women with exhausted eyes – that exhaustion she knows.

Mary understands that everyone around her is infirm in some way. They hold each other as if they are old friends. Immediately ahead is a group of lepers, the rags around their necks as rotted as their extremities. She can't bear to look at them and she is distressed by the sound of the bells tied to their waists, warning the populace to move out of the way. But how can you move out of the way when you cannot move at all, because the crush of people is so heavy?

She speaks to a woman with a bleeding condition, who has been waiting since the day before to speak to the Christ. Mary asks how long she has suffered from the issue of blood. Twelve years, says the woman. The blood is unceasing, small amounts that leak from her at every moment of every day. From where, asks Mary, and immediately wants to take the question back. It is too close a thing to ask of a stranger. But the woman smiles shyly and hopelessly and drops her voice to say the bleeding occurs in her female parts. She is a woman alone, her belongings tied in a cloth on her back. Once a prominent family, she has spent all her money on physicians. No one was able to cure her and so she is here. She has been told that the man they call the Christ will heal her, if only she asks. As she listens to the woman, Mary thinks her own complaint is not so urgent after all. She may be a bleeder too, but only from the mind, from the eyes, from the invisible parts. It is something to be grateful for.

She can always tell where he is. If she goes to the noisiest part of the crowd she can be sure he is somewhere at the centre of the disturbance. How does he live with it? Does he not grow tired? She is tired just from being near him, but she is no longer crying. A strange kind of happiness has come to her. She thinks she has exhausted her sad cells and opened up the happy ones. She lets the crowd carry her towards him and away from him. She does nothing but let herself be carried. Sooner or later she will be carried to him, she knows.

And then she sees the woman she had spoken to, who has been bleeding for twelve years. The woman approaches the Christ but is unable to get close enough. She touches the hem of his robe. In that surging crowd she stands absolutely still, her eyes closed and her face turned up to the sky. He asks who it was that touched him. The foolish men who accompany him for their own reasons tell him nobody has touched him, or everybody has touched him.

There are so many people, what does he mean by asking who touched him?

'Someone touched,' he says. 'I felt the virtue leave me.'

When the woman hears this she falls to the ground. It was she, she says, because she has been sick for many years with the bleeding. Now it has stopped. She can feel it. He has healed her.

He says, it was not me, but your faith.

A murmur goes through the spectators. Soon there is a great laying of hands. The sick and the insane begging for a touch. Each time someone reaches for him and the fingers close around his wrist or arm or ankle, some essence is taken out of him. He is depleted. He slumps into himself and covers his head with his hands. The sky changes colour. To the west, flattened clouds roll towards the sea.

A strange woman is wailing in a language no one can understand. Someone says it is Greek. It is not, says a bearded giant of a man, it is Syrophoenician or maybe Persian. The giant takes a few strides into the crowd and translates the woman's cries. He says the wailing woman has a young daughter who was overtaken by an unclean spirit. She asks that the Lord cast out the spirit. The Christ is on the ground cross-legged. He is covering his face. No, he says. He is tired unto death. He has had no food, not a sip of water. He has been healing the sick for days. Where are the children? They should be healed first. It is wrong to take the bread from the children and cast it to the dogs. Some wild hope enters the woman's face. She ululates a feverish string of words, which the smiling giant translates. Yes, she says, yes, Lord, it is wrong. But the dogs under the table eat from the children's crumbs. He seems to like

98

her answer. He tells the woman to go her way. He tells her the devil has gone out of her daughter. She is at home, peaceably sleeping.

Mary wonders what kind of devil the young woman harboured. Was it the same devil of sadness that had been with her? Where has it gone, to whom? The devils are finite in number and when they leave one of us they enter another. She stands up and folds her cloak around her, a bulwark against the devils in the desert that enter the nostrils as sand and leave through the eyes. And against the devils in the air that enter the lungs and grow into the heart. She is her own bulwark. She watches the woman walk home to her daughter and she knows they will be safe. But how long before the devils are loosed again?

'This is the great undoing,' the giant says tenderly. 'Everything that was done will be undone.'

The spectators grow quiet. A flat cloud sails in front of the sun and blots out the light. The wind turns cold. It is fitting weather for the end of the day and the end of the world. As the sunlight fades, so does the crowd. For the first time in months a smile appears on Mary's face. She buys a flagon of sour wine from a man whose wares are placed on a blanket on the ground and she pours a cup for the Christ. He accepts and takes a small sip and sighs. With this gesture she knows herself as one of them.

And when they see there is a woman among the disciples, others join, Joanna, wife of Chuza, and Susanna, and those who come at the end, but first there was Mary of Magdala.

# 13

I felt the nails go in and I heard the sound they made inside my bones. I felt the parch on my lips and I asked for water and though no sound left me someone soaked a sponge with sour wine and put it on a sprig of hyssop and held it to my mouth. The blood in my eyes made it difficult to see but I knew it was you, Mary. I knew it was you and I sipped at the sponge, not to ease the pain, no wine would ease it, but to be fully awake in the breaking and to know the shape the nails made inside me. Below me I saw you, Mary. And I saw my mother, whom I had set at a great distance from me. I saw that my true disciples had never left me. Mary my mother and Mary of Magdala. I heard you ask the watchers if you could give me a drop more of the sour wine to moisten the cracks on my lips and I heard them tell you no and I heard the breath that left you when they said you would be taken from the hill by force. What I said then I said for you, to say to the twelve brothers of weakness who left me in my hour of need. Write, Mary. I say to them it is not finished, nor will it be finished until the dry lands become water and the water becomes dry and the battle rages between the usurers and the usurpers, until it rages on the plains and the hills and the floods come again. I say to them to heed as the battle is already upon them. The lure is upon all men. I cannot speak more, for my body has gone away from me. And then you came, Mary, with a sponge to clean my legs and put a drop of oil on my feet as you had done in the life where I was whole, even as some among the watchers commanded you to stop and I told you to stop also, for I want you to listen as I say to you that forgiveness is the recourse of the weak and we are not weak and we must not forgive.

# 14

It is only a head, smaller than it was in life. The air has gone out of him. The lies and pride that puffed him up are gone and here is the head on a bed of figs, served for the amusement of her guests.

Unlike her husband she has grown accustomed to the sight of blood. She has come to enjoy it. A family weakness. Her mother was spared her grandfather's blood justice. But her father was not and her grandmother was not, and so many of her uncles that she has lost count. When it was time for her to marry she did as her mother told her and kept her sights within the family. Her first husband was the wrong uncle Herod. First they lived in Judaea and then they moved to Rome, where she hoped he would work himself into the Emperor's graces. He did not. Her regard for him dissolved into indifference when she found him one morning in the servants' quarters playing the flute, or trying to play, having appointed a shepherd boy his master. She knew in that instant that he would never be King. He would always be an underling, a sub-king, one of half a dozen witless men at the far periphery of power.

She stopped participating in the life of the court. She stayed in her chambers, waited upon by her maids. When he came to the door to ask what was wrong, he was not allowed in. She heard him berating her handmaiden, though he did not say a word to her. One afternoon she sent for him. When he arrived, flustered, because he had not seen her in twenty days, he found her on the bed and her handmaiden beside her. She allowed him to mount her, if only at the correct time of month as calculated by the midwife. Not long after the morning of the flutes she became pregnant by the wrong Herod. It was the right child, her Salomé, both cousin and daughter, who loved her mother. Her lovely child would grow up to have her eyes and hips, and she would be unblessed by ambition or cleverness. Salomé was the only one of her first husband's gifts that she wished to keep. A year after the birth of her daughter she began to lose some of the plumpness she had acquired when she was nursing. Her husband's brother and wife came to Rome to stay with them. When did she know that this was the right Herod, the uncle she should have married in the first place? It might have been on the first night at the feast they held for Herod Antipas and his silent wife. It might have been when she instructed the meat be passed to him and found his eyes lingering upon her. He was the Tetrarch, already more than her Herod would ever be. They divorced their spouses and married each other. It was ordained, she told him. It should have been this way from the start.

The marriage was made out of the raw materials of power. When mixed with good sense and affection, it proved to be stronger than love. There were some among the people who understood the meaning of their union, visionaries who called themselves the Herodians and hoped that she and her new husband would make their long-whispered dream come true – a Jewish kingdom separate from the empire of Rome. She would arrive unannounced, with a retinue, to their secret meetings. She would leave her cloak on and speak a few well-chosen phrases. After all, what right do they have to rule us? By whose sanction? What right do they have over a true princess of the Hasmonean line, the only daughter of Berenice and granddaughter to the Great Herod? She would remind them that though her husband was Idumean, he was son to the Great Herod, and named after his fearsome father. Finally, before she left, pale, heroic, her voice trembling, she would tell them to remember who they were: the Herodians, sole guardians of the Jewish kingdom.

Those who condemned them, she condemned in turn as backward tribespeople still living under the shadow of Moses, barbarians driven by low intelligence and high passion. Chief among their tormentors she counted the Baptiser, the loathsome man who questioned her marriage and called it unlawful. It angered her that he had dared to pass judgement. He had called a queen unlawful. For she *was* the Queen. The Romans addressed her as the Tetrarch's wife but in Galilee she was Queen and her husband was not Tetrarch but King. She wanted the Baptiser beheaded without delay, without trial. Her husband had him arrested and thrown into prison, but he would go no further. The King feared the anger of the people. He had not learned that the emotions of the populace could be directed anywhere a ruler wished. She knew because she had been a favourite of her grandfather. A clever king when it came to shaping opinion and doing away with those who wished him harm. She had learned cleverness from a master.

'Kill him,' she told her husband. 'I want his head impaled on your oldest and dullest sword.'

He would not do it. He was too polite.

As the days passed her anger only grew. It led to one of the few times that she and her husband were not in agreement about the course of their life together. She said the Baptiser must not be allowed to go free. It would be a sign of weakness on their part that a critic of their union, which was the very basis of their power, had been allowed to say such things about them.

'You don't like him as a man,' her husband said.

'Men should be useful if they want to be liked,' she replied. 'And anyway, you like him more than you like me.'

He did not deny it. Instead, he laughed. And there she left it. There was nothing to be gained by argument.

For his name day they invite the most prominent men of the realm, the lords and high captains who are ill at ease in the finery of the Queen's dining room. She has planned a surprise. With the wine there will be an entertainment, some music and a dance. Only then will the banquet be served. She waits until after Herod has had his bath before she goes to him.

'I must tell you my dream,' she says.

'Are you still dreaming of floods in the desert?'

'It rained all night. When it rains I dream.'

'Tell me,' says the King. 'Tell me the dream, that I might know its meaning.'

The images are fresh in her mind. She tells of a great city by the sea and the towers of learning that rise to the sky and the students who live and study there. The blight that comes unannounced. The dead unearthed from their graves. The burial chambers emptied. The dry ground fed with blood. And the worst part of the dream, the thing she cannot forget. The King sent into exile, forced to wander from one hostile town to the next.

'And what about the Queen?' says Herod. 'What happens to her?'

'I follow you to a place of two rivers where we both shall die.'

'Then I won't complain,' he says.

This small thing makes her sad but only for a moment. Today is the day a small part of the debt that is owed to them will be repaid.

'Salomé has a gift for your name day,' she tells him. 'She will dance for the guests but really it is only for you.'

Immediately his mood improves. Salomé is his favourite. They have no children of their own and she is the closest he has to an heir. He has never seen her dance. He knows that she has been studying with the dancing girls since she was a child, under the teacher with the long white hair and black eyes, who is seen sometimes wandering around the palace like a ghost. Soon Salomé will marry a cousin or uncle and then she will leave. A distressing thought he puts out of his mind. Today is his name day.

It is already dark when the Queen leaves her husband to check on the arrangements. The lamps have been lit and a carpet laid from the front gates across the great courtyard to each of the main hall's six entrances. The King's men have taken up their positions along the wall. She has ordered five hundred oil lamps placed in rows through the courtyard and around the porch. She checks the guards' uniforms and headgear and calls for more scarlet among the flowers on the tables and the banners on the wall. She has arranged for masses of scarlet and crimson on every surface. On her way out she inspects the musicians. A singer is running through her scales and a harpist is setting up his ungainly instrument in the centre of the room. The powdered anti-mony with which he has outlined his eyes has flaked onto his cheeks. She tells her assistant to make sure it is corrected.

Her daughter is already dressed in the sheer red tunic she will dance in. It is gathered at the neck by a delicate gold clasp. She notices how long the girl's hair has become, how lustrous and thick, how much like her own when she wears it open. She inspects her daughter's face for flaws. Salomé's eyes are too big but this cannot be helped. She applies some scarlet to deepen the unpleasing thinness of her lips. Then she perfumes the girl's hair and clavicles and wrists and ankles.

'How old are you now?'

Her daughter says, 'I am fifteen and a half, Mother.'

'Don't call me that,' she says. 'You know how much I loathe it. Call me your Queen, like everyone else.'

Already so old, she thinks. But at least she knows how to use her hips in dance and in life. At least she has learned to flatter and charm. Tonight she will learn how to use the power of her eyes to bend a man and break him. She will learn how to earn his thanks in the breaking. It is the most important lesson she will take from her mother.

From her daughter's room she retires to her own, where she finishes her toilet quickly and perfumes herself and adorns her hair. She is in the hall as the guests arrive and the wine is poured and drunk. Toasts are made to the health of the King. She gives the signal and the Herodians present a song they have composed, four voices cloistered in harmony. Then there is a speech by an elder about the wonderful things the King has done. He praises his majesty's great creation, the city of Tiberias. The springs that cure any ailment of the skin and heal all scabs and ulcers. The water that boils without the need for fire. Soon, the elder says, the city will be ritually cleansed and then it will become a great centre of learning. More wine is served, a new wine fit for the soldier's palate. Another toast is drunk to the continued health of Herod Antipas. The fervent young Herodians reach the climax of their song. *We shall be released, our blood, our soil, our King.*

The Queen claps her hands. Her excitement makes her dizzy. She is never sure of the sequence of events that follow, or what was actually said. What she remembers most clearly is the way she holds her breath during her daughter's dance.

The attendants bring in a banquet table and place it in the centre of the room directly before the King. On the long table is Salomé, reclining as if she has died and it is her wake. There are orange slices on her eyes and a small bunch of black grapes on her mouth and figs and pomegranates on her body, arranged around a deep bowl of honey. She rests against a bed of scarlet leaves from the sumac tree. The leaves have been twined into her hair and fashioned into anklets and bracelets for her wrists. The guests are invited to pick a morsel here or a morsel there. But only the King may take the orange slices from her eyes and the grapes that obscure her smiling mouth. As she is slowly revealed, the guests notice that her toes and fingertips and lips have been coloured with a subtle crimson dye.

When the fruit has all been taken and eaten, her eyes open and she sits up very slowly. Her carmine tunic is stained with the juice of the grape and the crushed sumac. Very slowly, so slowly that it hurts to watch, she lifts her left foot with both hands and places it behind her neck. The King gapes. Though the move seems to take a great length of time, no one is aware of time passing except the wine bearers, who must make sure the cups are full. They have been told to keep their eyes averted from the dance. Then, slower still, each breath the length of a glacial age, her right foot also finds the back of her neck until she is balanced only on her hands. Twisted thus, precariously balanced so that a puff of breath would topple her, she turns herself a quarter way round until her back is to the King.

The room has fallen silent. The lords and commanders are frozen into their positions at the table. She makes it look comfortable, the impossible shape her body has taken. It is only when they look closely that they see the strain on her face and the imperceptible breathing. With her legs lifted and parted and locked into place, she is the picture of female desire. And each of the guests suddenly understands the meaning of slowness. They understand that if you think of time as a shapeable thing, then that is what it becomes. Your pet and your slave. They understand what it means to be master of your body, every blood vessel and beat, to be the kind of person who commands time and the body into slowness.

There is a pause the length of another glacial age. She makes one more quarter turn and then another, the final turn, which leaves her facing the King at last, her eyes on his, her weight balanced on her palms, her small body folded into the unnatural shape. Just as it seems she will fall, she disengages her feet. First the right and then the left, slowly, mindfully. And she is on her knees, bowing deeply to the man whose name day it is.

The guests have not said a word during the performance. They haven't moved. Some have stopped breathing. Now they erupt into shouted applause. There is the sound of chairs scraping on the floor and relieved laughter. But the King appears frozen into displeasure, as if he has seen the end of the world and the end of his reign, the dissolution of his flesh and the flesh of those he loves. Mother and daughter watch Herod Antipas rise to his feet and gesture for silence.

'Whatever there is,' he says, 'whatever you want, speak and it is yours. This is my oath as King and Tetrarch of the territories of Galilee and Perea.'

Salomé stays on her knees. Her head is bowed and her eyes closed, the red-tipped hands braced on either side of her.

'Whatever you wish for is yours,' says the King, his eyes moist.

She steps from the table and walks barefoot across the red stone floors to her mother. Mother and daughter whisper together for a long time, an urgent back and forth. Then, very slowly, as if she were still in the grip of the performance, Salomé turns to the King and asks for the head of the Baptiser. She wants it dressed in the kitchen and brought to her on a platter. There is more laughter from the guests and shouts of approval. The Queen demands silence.

'Ask for something else. Anything else,' says the King. 'Not this.'

But her good daughter insists on the terms of the arrangement. She reminds him that he said he would give her anything she wants. And this is what she wants, the head of John. Won't you give it to me? she says, falling to her knees, her great eyes imploring the King. The guests watch silently, unwilling to interrupt the sudden turn of events. When Herod gives the order to his guards to rouse the executioner it seems entirely in keeping with the day. The Queen sighs: a sound of pure contentment.

The executioner is a soft-spoken man with a terrible hangover. He mutters quietly as he sets about to find a hand-saw and two assistants to hold the prisoner down. John, told that Salomé has asked for his head, is on his knees when the men arrive. There is a woman crouched by the bars of the cell talking to him in urgent tones and imploring him about something. They make her leave. The assistants hold him while the executioner saws at his dirt-encrusted neck. At first John does not make a sound, because he has sworn to remain silent. But when the saw cuts into his spine he screams and they call for more guards. He is unexpectedly strong for an old man. His scream becomes a bellow and his struggles continue until a last column of bone is revealed. The saw, unable to find purchase, catches on the meat of his shoulder. The men who hold him are gummy with blood. When it is done they take the head to the kitchen, the Baptiser's long hair hanging from the executioner's fist. The head is washed and dressed and placed on a silver platter with a necklace of figs and sumac leaves. Two cooks take the platter to the King, who gestures to his stepdaughter. She takes it around the room to the grunts and applause of the guests. The chief estates of Galilee are pleased.

They notice that Salomé's eyes are glassy with emotion for the first time that evening. Perhaps she is horrified at what she has done and is unable to look at the bloody platter in her arms. But then she puts the dish down and takes a pin from her mother and uses it to secure the Baptiser's protruding tongue to one place. She says something to her mother that the guests strain to hear and cannot.

Much later when news of the Christ comes to Galilee, Herod Antipas is convinced it is the Baptiser. He is alive and returned for vengeance. No amount of reason or argument by his courtiers will convince the Idumean that the man is dead. She reminds him that the Baptiser's head was conclusively separated from his body and presented to the court at dinner. She reminds him of the way the man's tongue stuck out of his mouth. She reminds him of her words at the sight, *insolence beyond death.* That she had to summon the cook to cut off his tongue and give it to her as a keepsake, the tongue that had caused so much royal anguish. But none of this matters. As far as Herod knows, the Baptiser's head has somehow returned to his other parts and he is there among the people, raising the dead, curing the incurable. Each questionable miracle confirms that heaven and hell do in fact exist. She is unable to make her husband believe otherwise.

Soon her dream of prophecy comes true. Her husband is exiled to Lugdunum. The new king, her brother, allows her to remain in Galilee. But she chooses to follow her husband to the shores of a new land where they will live and quietly die.

She is Herodias, wife of Herod Antipas and mother of Salomé.

# 15

Now she remembers only the dance, how long it was, longer than any she had attempted. She remembers how hard her mother made her work. I want you to imagine you are pregnant, her mother said, imagine the horror of the birthing. For it is a horror, with no reward except a mewling that swallows up the best years of your life. Imagine and create a dance that will make every man in the room hold his breath.

She worked with the dance mistress for close to a year. The length of time, her mother said, that it took to birth a baby. She did not study long with the dancing girls, because they knew only to flash their eyes and this was not what her mother had in mind. She took lessons from the juggler and the magician, but she learned most from the contortionist and the old dance mistress. Because she was young she could do things they could not. But they taught her how to slow her breathing, how to inhabit the blood in her veins and the pores on her skin, and how to mould her limbs into positions that seemed impossible without causing damage to the nerves and joints. These are the things her mother brought her.

Her mother. It was still strange to think of the woman as anyone's mother. She didn't know her until she was eight years of age. Before her second name day, Herodias had sent her to live with a succession of cousins and aunts whilst she and her new husband travelled between Galilee and Judaea and Rome. In her mother's words they were 'cultivating the Roman fields' and 'planting seeds for future harvests'. All she knew about her mother was that she was a Hasmonean princess. She was beautiful and rich. She had named her daughter after her own grandmother and her life was too busy to accommodate a small child.

Salomé was sent to live with her aunt, who took the motherless girl to her bosom. This aunt, whom she called mother, was the only one in her life with whom she came to feel any kind of family bond. It grew stronger as her aunt grew older and stranger. Each morning she would speak in a tongue no one understood to people who were not there. Sometimes it sounded as if she were haranguing her invisible companions and at other times it seemed she was being harangued. There were times when the arguments would turn physical and she would find her aunt on the floor, wrestling with unseen shapes. At these times her aunt would cry the name of a man and cough as if something was lodged in her throat.

The man her aunt hated more than any other was a distant uncle related by marriage, who spread the story that it was she who had ordered the beheadings of her husband's enemies. Because she enjoyed watching, she would ask that it was carried out slowly, and she insisted viewers get close enough to be stained by the spatter. The stories were true, but the spreading of them and the tone in which the uncle spoke about her, this she objected to. When the uncle who spread the true stories died, she asked that his body be sent to her court so they might pay their respects. The body arrived in a day, already stinking in the heat. She inhaled deeply and gazed at her uncle's face. His head had shrunken in death and the scalp had ridged into the texture of a dried plum. The skin on his face appeared puckered and scaled. The dilated nostrils had been stuffed with stained cotton balls. She ordered that the body be thrown to the crocodiles and his head brought to her on a simple wooden platter.

'How nice it is to see you in your highest state,' her aunt said to the head. Pulling out the man's shrunken tongue she pierced it with a carving knife that she pinned to the platter on which the head was secured. She said, 'How nice to see your sharp tongue receive its proper rebuke.'

Her aunt looked around the court and noticed the expression on the faces of her friends. She laughed then and led them in applause. It was the first time the girl had seen her aunt laugh. The sweetness of her laughter, as if she were a little girl again, made her feel a sudden affection for her eccentric relative. When her aunt died of apoplexy the following year she was stricken in a way she was not when she heard of the deaths of her mother and stepfather many years later.

After her aunt's death the girl was sent to live with the family of a great-uncle, whose son she grew to detest. They were almost of the same age yet he acted as if he was much older. On her first day at the new house she wandered around the rooms without seeing them. Then she went to the back courtyard and stared at the packed dirt. She tried to draw with a branch a picture of her dead aunt's extraordinary face.

Her cousin found her there and pulled her to her feet. Without saying a word he drove his fist into her stomach. When he saw the tears in her eyes he was satisfied. From then on whenever he found her alone he would strike her, or twist her hair around his fist, or take from her whatever was in her hands. Only when he saw her tears would he stop tormenting her. It became a ritual between them. He would hurt her in ways that became increasingly gentle and she would cry and they would separate, satisfied, though neither could have put into words why this was so.

When her mother sent for her she was reluctant to leave her great-uncle's house and her cousin, even if they rarely spoke. She did not understand why she was to go to an unknown house in Galilee to be with people she did not care for. She could not recall anything of her mother or the man they called the Tetrarch and she was full of anger that other people controlled her comings and goings. She was thirteen, past the age at which a girl must get married. Her only wish was to find a husband as quickly as possible and live in her own house.

In the house in Galilee she learned to be quiet and to keep her opinions to herself. She learned to stay out of the way of her parents, particularly when they were discussing something in low voices. She was taught by a succession of masters but only the teaching of the dance and the sword stayed with her. The sword masters taught her balance and how to trust her senses. She felt a sense of control for the first time. Among the dance teachers she was drawn to a woman with long white hair and black-rimmed eyes who did not teach dance at all. Her first concern was that the girl should learn how to breathe. She insisted that it was not movement she was interested in teaching, but how to eat correctly, how to dress, how to use your eyes and lips and accept the body's demands, and what to demand in return. The lessons in breathing helped her stay calm when speaking to her mother and helped still the anger that choked her sometimes for no reason at all. The woman took a month to teach her to sit and a month to teach her to stand and a year or more to teach her emptiness, so that the bones in her feet and the joints in her knees were nothing more than a means to moments of perfect stillness when she could be anything, a green snake twined around a column, or a cat curled into itself, or an unmoving self-sustaining system animated only by consciousness.

She had been studying with the dance mistress for two years when her mother told her she would dance on the name day of the King. Her mother didn't care what kind of dance it was, as long as it was pleasing and arduous and she looked the King in the eyes. She and the mistress created a dance that altered the viewer's conception of time. Each movement took so long that nobody watching was conscious of the hour of the day, or where they were, or why. Watching the dance was almost as arduous and physically demanding as performing it. For much of the hour and fifteen minutes it took to endure she was bent backwards or bent double. The only constant was that her legs were parted and her thighs open to the viewer and her sex obscured by a fold of scarlet cloth.

At the end of the dance she broke eye contact with the King and bowed low from the waist. She brought her hands together to signal that the performance was finished and the entire court seemed to let out a single breath. The usual noises began, the usual applause, servants moving among the tables and people coughing, the sound of cutlery striking wood, exclamations of surprise and delight and men of high estate demanding more wine. Then the King got to his feet and called for silence. He swore in front of his guests that whatever she wished for, he would give her. All she had to do was ask.

Barefoot she climbed down from the table on which she had been dancing and barefoot she walked across the red stone tiles to her mother. The two women whispered together.

'Tell him you want the Baptiser brought up from the dungeons and brought to us here. Tell him you want to see the man whipped for his insolence.'

She smiled kindly at her mother.

'Is that all you want?' she said.

'Tell him,' said her mother.

'Don't you want something more?'

'Tell him what I told you to say.'

The girl turned to the King and said:

'Bring me someone's head on a big dinner plate.'

'Someone's head?' the King faltered.

'Yes,' said the girl, laughing. 'A big head on a big plate.'

The King said, 'Whose head have you set your mind upon?'

She inclined her face to her mother, for she had forgotten the man's name. Her surprised mother whispered in her ear. Such an inoffensive name. The ordinary name of an ordinary man. She would not say it. She did not want to know it.

'The Baptiser,' she told the King. She waited for the hubbub to die down. 'I want his head on a fresh platter.'

'Ask for something else. Anything else,' said the King. 'Not this.'

'But this is what I want.'

'Riches, a retinue of slaves, a share of my kingdom. Whatever you want. Not this.'

She put her great eyes on his. The eyes that had learned their purpose from a mistress of the body arts. She said:

'Won't you give it to me?'

The King shook his head.

'You gave me your oath. Everyone heard.'

She waited, bored and impatient at her mother's side until a man's head was brought and placed on a low table. The eyes were crusted over. The neck wound still dripped its muck on the plate. The expression on his face, what was it? Not fear, but amusement. The boredom she had felt a moment ago was replaced by surprise. How was he still laughing at them, at her? Wide awake, she remembered her beloved aunt and asked her mother for a hairpin. She was not wearing one. Her hair had been left loose for the dance. Her mother took a pin out of her own abundant hair. A long pin with an ivory clasp. She fished out the dead man's tongue and pulled at it with both hands. Girlishly she looked around at the men assembled at the great tables, the powerful men who commanded her stepfather's armies. Addressing the Baptiser, she asked why he was laughing. Wagging his tongue up and down, she said, 'Oh, are you trying to say something?' She pierced her mother's hairpin through and stuck it deep into the wood of the table. The dead man's tongue was coated with something white and slippery. For some mad reason he was still amused, even if he had fallen silent.

Speaking under her breath she told her mother, 'Now he will never again speak ill of you.'

The King asked if she knew the man's name.

'Of course I do,' the girl replied, 'he is the Baptiser.'

'No,' said the King. 'His name is John.'

She smiled and counted her breaths. When she counted to three, the name was forgotten. She opened her dry eyes and thanked the King for his generosity.

When she remembers her stepfather it is without emotion. If she thinks of her mother at all, she recalls the actions of a stranger who held some great sway over her for a brief moment in her girlhood. She remembers her instructions. To make a dance as if she were making a child. How hungry the woman was for power. What had it brought her except an exile's grave in a faraway country?

Now she is the Queen and she is better suited to rule than her mother. She knows to mask her intentions. Her first marriage to a much older uncle, a Tetrarch like her stepfather, did not last long. Her husband became quickly feeble and conducted most of the court business from his chamber. He rarely left his bed, not even to eat or bathe. She helped him with his duties and made the decisions he would not, or could not. By the time of his death she had long passed the marriageable age for a girl, but she was the daughter of Herodias. A Hasmonean queen in her own right. When a proposal came she accepted without understanding that the man she was marrying was the cousin she had known as a girl, Aristobulus. He gave her the sons her elderly first husband could not. She does not dance but continues the exercises she learned from the white-haired mistress of her youth. If she does her daily exercises and doesn't touch alcohol and is mindful of her diet, she will live into healthy old age. She wants to be Queen for a long time. The first time her cousin tries to punch her in the stomach, as he had when they were children, she makes a fist and strikes him on the left ear with the point of her knuckles. His eyes cross and his head wobbles on the puny stalk of his neck. He has to sit down in the dust of the courtyard. He never strikes her again but complains that she has damaged his hearing. There is a constant ringing in his head that gets louder the older he gets. It makes him anxious at odd moments of the day, particularly when it is quiet. The ringing becomes so loud he cannot sleep.

'Why is it always so quiet?' Aristobulus complains one night. 'I can hear the dizzy leaking into my head.' And then he strikes at his forehead as if to dislodge a worm.

He does not like the quiet, she knows, and so she calls the servants.

'You are to go barefoot from now on,' she tells them. 'Do you understand?'

'Yes, my Queen,' they answer in unison.

'When you are in the halls of my house or anywhere in the vicinity of the King you are not to speak, never!'

'Yes, my Queen.'

'Do you know what will happen if you do not go barefoot? If you make the slightest sound while discharging your duties?'

'My Queen?'

'I will separate you from your feet. And what will happen if you speak? If you are not completely silent while creeping around the palace in your bare feet? Do you know?'

'You will separate us from our tongues?'

'Clever girl,' she tells the handmaiden who has spoken. Soon her husband will die. And so will she: winter holiday, thin ice.

Shalom or Salomé is her name, daughter of Herodias and Queen of Chalcis and Armenia Minor.

# 16

She does not see the dance but the aftermath.

Oil lamps burn in the courtyard, five hundred brass bowls holding five hundred wicks that must stay lit through the evening. The Queen says she wants her guests to walk through a field of light and she will tolerate only perfumed oil in the bowls. After issuing this instruction she disappears and leaves the actual labour to her. Two hours later some of the lamps run out of oil and must be replenished immediately. She moves four servants from the kitchen to the courtyard, where they will stand ready to refill the bowls from a great barrel of cypress oil hidden behind a screen of red linen. After the crisis of the oil lamps, her husband tells her there is a shortage of silver drinking cups. She must find more cups and place the better silver by the men closest to the King. For most of the next hour, bent over, she runs between the kitchen and the storerooms. Her husband keeps house for the King but she keeps house for her husband, which means she keeps house for the King even if her husband is the one charged with the task.

When the silver has been placed correctly and the wine cups filled and refilled she notices the excitement on the faces of some of the guests. Shalom is kneeling on the table on which she has danced, her head bowed, face hidden behind her open hair. The Queen's pleasure is plain to see, as is the King's distress. He has collapsed against the throne. His chin is propped in his hand and his feast day forgotten. When he issues the order for the head of the Baptiser she clutches her own throat in fear. The old man has been in the fortified palace's prison for a month and she has come to know him. Sometimes she takes him a plate of food from the kitchen. He always refuses meat and wine. He lives on bread, dry fruits and water. Only once does he mention her infirmity. She is bent almost double and has been that way for years. Each year the stoop gets worse. He tells her it is by reason of her work in a house defiled by the wicked.

Now she runs ahead of the King's guard when they go to find the Baptiser. He is sitting against the wall of a cell filthy with his own waste and his right leg is shackled to a post. Clutching the bars, she tells him to beg the King for pity.

'There is no pity,' says the Baptiser. He struggles to his knees to pray. 'Not from man and not from God.'

'Does not your God believe in pity and forgiveness?'

'He does not and that is why he is God,' the old man tells her. His lips are unexpectedly red in the brown leather of his face. 'Neither does your fox and that is why you call him King.'

When the men of the guard arrive they are escorting the executioner. He has been roused from his bed. A squat quiet man who reeks of strong wine, the executioner's eyes are bloodshot slits in his head. She notices the wounds on his knuckles and face, some yet to heal, and the sleep caked in his eyes. The only thing about him that seems well cared for is the saw he carries in his heavy fist.

Edrei, the chief of the guards, commands her to leave. It does not matter that she is the wife of Chuza, he says, she has no business being there. She should not speak with their prisoner.

'Yes,' says the old man, getting up. 'Let the cowards do their bloody work with no witness to speak of it.'

She sees how tall he is and how frail. But he speaks with great authority in a voice that must surely carry into the courtyard. She would like to share some words of comfort but the words don't come. She does not know how to take her leave of the old man. Edrei pulls her by the arm and moves her past the cells.

Outside she stands among the flickering lamps and hears a cry, or it might be the neighing of the tethered horses. In minutes the guard appears with the old man's head on a flat wooden charger. She follows them into the dining hall and watches as the daughter of Herodias desecrates his tongue with a hairpin. The King's discomfort is evident to all. He dismisses the assembled court with a clap of his hands. There will be no more speeches and no more entertainment. But the guests refuse to move. She returns to the kitchen and helps the servants with the washing of the utensils and the putting away of leftover food. When she picks up the tray of silver cups to return them to the storerooms, she finds the silver is heavier than it was earlier in the day. It makes her stoop more than usual. How deep will she bend before she folds in two and breaks?

Much later, the hall is still being cleared when some men arrive to take possession of the Baptiser's body. They go to the cell where the old man spent his last months and bring the corpse through the courtyard to the road. They find the head where it is pinned to a wooden platter and place it with the body. It is late at night. With the light of a torch she closes the old man's eyes and pushes the stump of his tongue into his mouth and closes it as securely as she can. She brings a basin of warm salt water to clean the body and severed head. The blood has hardened into lumps. She finds a jar of nard and carefully anoints him, then uses linen packed with aloes to wrap him from neck to foot. As she winds the linen around his neck he seems whole for a moment. But she knows he is not, nor will he ever be. Lastly she brings small scissors and trims his nails and beard and the matted long hair on his head. After the body is washed and dressed the men take him out on a wooden slab that acts as a makeshift bier. There are three of them, one no more than a child. It is inadequate manpower for any funeral but especially for the Baptiser, who is tall and heavy-boned. She joins them on an impulse, leaving the palace without a word to her husband. What would she say to him? What would be the use of it? None. There is no pity to be had from the fox she calls King and none from his steward her husband.

By the time they reach the city walls it is daybreak. The word has spread and their small group of four has become eight. She leads the procession. Though she is bent over, she is the only woman among them and she knows her duty. She has heard the elders say it enough times, that it is women who introduced death into the world and so it is women who must lead the funeral processions. The first time her grandmother told her this it struck her as wrong.

Women may bring death into the world but they also bring life. Should they not be rewarded? Her grandmother had looked at her for a moment in silence. Then she said it was better to hold one's tongue in the presence of one's elders.

The boy who is holding one end of the bier stumbles where the road gets rocky. The body shifts but does not fall. More mourners join them, women, who move to the front of the procession. Together they chant an elegy telling of the Baptiser:

> Our sons and daughters
> Washed in God's waters.

The elegy is a signal. A young woman tears at her robe and begins to wail. Immediately the other women join in. They have been forbidden to mourn the Baptiser's death but the Queen's order is forgotten once the singing begins.

> What laughter but madness?
> What joy but sadness?

At the tomb, hewn out of a rock on the far side of the hill, they place the old man's body on a shelf. Soon the other mourners leave, who joined them along the way. Only she is left with the three who came to Herod's. They sit outside until the sun is high in the sky and a fine skim of red dust has settled on their clothes. She watches a line of white pelicans glide towards the River Jordan until they become pouched specks to the east of the hills. She is thinking about the old man, how he always seemed to be in good humour, though he was chained to the floor of his cell. If you asked a question he would say what was in his head. He didn't care to be liked. He had come to be known in all of Israel for his ideas about God. Yet he told her God is without pity. Then why was he willing to die for the laws of a pitiless God? She would have liked to ask him.

The two men get up. The boy has fallen asleep and they wake him gently. When they tell her they are going to see the man called Jesus to give him the news about the Baptiser's death, she asks if she can go with them. It has been an anxious night and morning. She has left her home and her husband because of the death of a man who should not have died, who was executed on a woman's whim. She has no wish to go back.

As they leave she stops to pick up a handful of dirt, which she throws against the old man's tomb. The dirt leaves a red stain against the stone. We are dust, she says, and to dust we shall return. She does not know if she is speaking to the old man or to the God without pity or forgiveness. Or is she speaking to herself? As they walk through the heat of the day her stooped gait slows them down. The red dust and rubble of the hills gives way to clay as they near the plains. Once she looks up at the startling blue sky, but then her eyes fall to the ground that is her vista. The men share with her their food and they stop once for water and then they continue walking until the sun passes its zenith and the day begins to cool. Towards evening they come to a lake and a great press of people. Again and again she hears the name Jesus. He has been speaking to the multitude from a small boat tethered near the shore because the crush of people was too much to accommodate on land.

They find him on the shore with a group of men who place themselves between him and the people who want to speak to him or touch him or beg something of him. Some just want to look at him, those men and women who gaze in adoration. But there are also those who are angry, as if he has let them down. Everywhere there is excitement, especially among those who are near him. She notices that women are crying simply because he walks past, or says a few words. As if fame has made him more than a man and beyond the laws that govern other men, beyond death and the needs of the body.

When the men who buried the Baptiser tell the Christ that he has been executed on the order of Herod's wife and stepdaughter, his face becomes the face of an old man much like the old man who was beheaded. She is struck by the similarity. Their features are the same, lean and sunken, the skin like brown leather left a long time in the sun. Even their beards are alike, trimmed rough and close to the skin. The Christ is motionless for a long time. He gets up slowly, full of years, and steps into the boat and allows no one to come with him. He sets off for the far side of the lake. The people will not let him alone. They have come from towns and villages nearby and far away and they will not leave without getting what they came for, even if they do not know what this might be.

She follows the crowd along the shores of a lake that is so wide she cannot see the other side. Now it is dark and the wind is cold from the water and some among them have lit torches. Someone gives her a stick, which makes it easier for her to walk. She has lost her three companions of the morning. But there are so many people she does not feel alone or frightened. It has been two nights since she has been away from her home and she hopes never to go back. She is happy to remain this way for the rest of her life, with a staff in hand, stooped, not halt, following a man who may have more to offer than the insults offered by her previous employer, the Queen.

When they come within sight of him she stops, too shy to go forward. He is laying his hands on the sick who are everywhere, women white at the mouth and men without limbs or eyes. She is astonished there are so many afflicted by unnameable ailments. In the face of such calamity her own seems to diminish. At least she can talk and eat and move about in the world. At least her mind has not been affected by her condition. Suddenly, pushed by the crowd, she is in front of him. He beckons to her. Standing very close he lifts her shoulders while pressing the small of her back. She stands fully upright for the first time in more than ten years. Her back feels out of alignment. There are pains where before there was only stiffness. She takes a few steps and stammers her name. Her vision is no longer tied to the ground. She notices the trees and the breezes that ruffle the leaves and the faces of people who are staring at her.

She will follow him. She will not return to the house of defilement served by her husband, who has been enslaved by the Queen and her King. She will follow him, she thinks, wherever he may roam. In time she will be among the women who are with him in the last hours on Golgotha and beyond, to the tomb, and she will be among the first to witness his return.

Her name is Joanna, wife of Chuza.

# 17

Say it is the secret, Mary, from the end to the beginning, from the crucifixion to the birth. Say you are the great feminine. The virgin wife and the matron child. She who is barren, who made her handmaiden lie under her and take her husband's seed, and she whose sons are too many to count. Say I am the noise of the sun and the silence that is spoken. Say I am the utterance of a name on the lips of the lost and the sound of a name in the maze of the ear. If you body what is in you what you body will save you, if you do not body what is in you what you do not body will kill you. Thomas the feminine, the twin and sister, the secret inside the secret book, the put-away and hidden. The books they will call untrue because they are true and the truths they will call heresy because it casts them as heretics. Know they will shame your name because you are the future. They will say there is only one true church when there are as many as there are tongues upon the earth. They will fall upon the weak and take their extortion, for they are usurpers grown rich in the citadels of Rome. They will deplore you and call you heresy. Know it is the truth they wish to mutilate and suppress. Theirs is the true heresy. Write, Mary, write it down and seal it in a jar for those who will find it in two thousand years. Among them will be those with the eyes to read and the ears to hear. What is birth if it is not birth into yourself and what is rebirth if it is not rebirth from yourself and who are you if you are not who you become and where are you if you are not here and why are you hastening if you are not hastening to be released? And I say this to you and you and all who follow. When they say that a gulf separates you from God, tell them they are doing the work of Satan. The self and God are the same. There is no heaven or hell, only the light of understanding and the veil of ignorance. There is no sin, only confusion. There is no guilt, only melancholy and there is no repentance, only acceptance. I came to you as guide, not master. When you drink from the drink that is in my mouth, the knowledge that is Apocrypha will open to you as I open to you. Listen, Mary, write. Those in the east who do not eat living creatures and those in the south who drink the blood of cattle and those in the west who eat only that which is cooked and those in the north who eat everything that moves, all are as human and divine as you. A taste of sour wine in the hyssop, a prayer from my mother whose forgiveness I beg, and a word from you, Mary, and now the pain is a wisp inside my feet. The memory of iron inside my wrists. I say this, Mary, to you, and ask that you say it to them.

# 18

As the youngest of seven brothers and sisters, and his father's favourite, he is not given a chance to speak when the family gathers. There are too many voices eager to drown him out. Mary listens intently if he has something to say but the others pay him no mind. This may be why he talks so much now and why he has never been well disposed to his brothers and sisters. They did not listen to him when he was a child. Now that he is older and fame rests upon him like a shiny new garment and all kinds of people follow him, examining his every word, sifting and sifting as if precious metals were buried therein – now he has no time for his family. When she or her brothers try to meet him, they are rebuffed, or they are made to wait with the mad and the dying and the army of the sick that follows him. Surrounded by chance figures and acquaintances picked up on the road, he behaves as if they are the strangers, his blood family, and not even the best among strangers.

Some time earlier there was to be a family wedding in Cana. She, Joses and Jude decided they would set off to find him and invite him to the wedding. When Mary heard them talking she said she would go too. They did not object.

If his loving mother was among them surely he would meet with his sister and brothers? Never having been to one of his gatherings, they were shocked by the size of the crowd and the noise and revelry and tears.

Joses made a joke, 'The moment he starts speaking, watch, all of these people will disappear.'

They all laughed. But then she saw Mary's pained expression and abruptly her laughter died.

'The moment he starts speaking they'll be running for the hills,' said Jude, clapping his older brother on the shoulder.

'They'll be running so fast we'll have to get out of the way,' said Joses, who considered himself the joker in the family. 'Or we'll be trampled! We'll be flattened!'

Her brothers whooped but in a half-hearted way. Because by then the crowd was thick and so unruly that being trampled or flattened was a possibility.

They never got to meet him. They got a glimpse of him from a far distance. He made them wait for no reason or perhaps it was to prove something to his followers. They sat on the ground while the light left the sky and the night turned cold and still they waited. He refused to meet them. He made a lesson out of them and made up the sayings the people around him loved to repeat. All men and women are my brothers and sisters. Whoever knows the word of God is my family. My mother is not my mother, as my father is not my father. Your family is made, not born. What need have I of sisters, are you not my sister? And so on. The seductive phrases designed to win him more fame and more followers. As if he needed more. There was no one in the world more famous, not the Tetrarch, not the Governor, not the Emperor of Rome. Eventually they turned back and went home and walked on unfamiliar roads for most of the way. Even her brothers were silent. Poor Mary was distraught, the lines on her face made deep. As it turned out, the expedition was in vain. Jesus received his own invitation to the wedding in Cana and he accepted.

She and he were the closest at one time, yet he behaved as if he did not know her. At the wedding when she got near enough to speak to him he would not meet her eye. He would not respond when she called him by name, *Jesu*, as she used to when they were children. Whatever she said, however warmly she tried to remind him of their shared childhood, he would not look at her or address her. When he did speak it was to everyone, as if his words were too precious to waste on one person. Sometimes he looked past her or through her as if she did not exist. As if his fame had deposited him somewhere remote, on a crag of rock far above the rest.

She kept count of the changes in him.

One, his eyes were always narrowed and squinting into the distance, as if the thing he sought was far away, invisible to those around him. Two, his clothes were different. Lately he had begun to wear an embroidered robe tied with a purple and scarlet sash. No fisherman or carpenter wore that kind of robe. It set him apart from the people who came to see him and the men who travelled with him. Three, his love was changeable. He loved only those who loved him. Most beloved to him were those men, and there were many, who welcomed him as the Christ. Their regard for him was indistinguishable from worship. Four, when he spoke to a group it was different from when he spoke to one person. If he was speaking to a single individual his manner was light and there were moments of amusement, even whimsy. But when he spoke to a crowd he was changed. His voice became softer and more powerful at the same time. The smile disappeared, and the humour, as if he wished to be remarked upon only for his seriousness. He was already thinking about the chroniclers of the future and how they would portray him. Sometimes he was sarcastic but never light-hearted. Five, he used silence as a tool or a weapon to shield himself against those who followed his every move. If he did not want to answer a question he would say nothing and the silence was so crushing that the questioner's face would fall. There would be discomfort all around, which seemed to satisfy him.

He left home in search of fame and it arrived with such ferocity that no one could have expected it. No one but he. When he was a child and she asked him why he did not join at mealtimes but preferred to eat alone, he would only shake his head. And he was always silent when his brothers asked when he would take up the tools of his father's trade. Only once did she remember him being driven to anger by their questions and taunts. He said:

'I will not apprentice myself to a carpenter because I am already apprenticed.'

'To what?' someone asked.

'To the future,' he replied. 'I am an apprentice to the future.'

He always knew he would be famous and, knowing this, he set himself apart at an early age. He knew it as a child and prepared for it. The story of his life he changed as he saw fit and left out the fact that he had a real family, real brothers and sisters and a mother who doted on him so much she ruined him. That he grew up in a home that may not have had many luxuries but at least they were never short of food or shelter. He likes to spread the idea that he appeared out of the sky like a bolt of lightning or fell from a distant star into the midst of a family in Galilee that knew nothing of him and did not deserve his beauty or his brilliance. It is not true. If anyone deserves him, it is she and his mother.

She thinks nothing of the fame or of the stories he plucks out of the air until much later, after he starts to travel the countryside stirring up trouble and people begin spreading their own stories about him. He walks on water like a two-legged fish and flies the sky like a wingless bird. He does not eat and drink like other men but finds his sustenance in the sunlight and in drops of rain. His hands are touched with a colourless light that makes green shoots sprout where there was nothing but dirt. They are welcome to their fantasies. It has nothing to do with her except as a source of family lore. But then some of his men write the stories down and turn them into gospels in which his brothers are mentioned by name and his sisters are not. She and Lydia are never named. They are hidden away like shameful family secrets. Two of her brothers also write popular versions of his life, James first, then Jude, and she and her sister are left out.

This is why, years later when the events of his life have been told in a hundred different ways, she is at the gates of the old city selling keepsakes of her childhood. On the near side of the gate a man leans against the stone, picking his teeth. He has been there since she arrived and all he has done, as far as she can tell, is watch her and pick his teeth. Perhaps he's thinking of buying something and can't make up his mind. She is a vendor of stories. People will pick up an item and demand to know where it came from. She always has a story ready, sometimes true. It is a way of taking part in the tales that have multiplied around him and a way of honouring her life and her sister's. Most of all, it is a way to earn a living. She is a poor woman, a widow in the world. And after all she is a part of the story and so is her poor sister. Considering all the false stories around him, would not his acolytes be interested in hearing something true or partly true? There are as many stories as there are people. Why shouldn't her stories occupy a moment of a stranger's attention?

On a striped blanket, brightly coloured to attract the attention of passers-by, she has placed her wares, grouped by species. She makes them in the evening and works quickly by candlelight. Animal figures made out of straw and cotton, a lamb, a goat, camels, horses, always a donkey or two. And lately she has begun to make birds – owls, but also falcons and turtledoves. She will add a tear and some dirt on a paw, or she will drop a stitch and put in an eye, only to tear it out. She tells those who stop that the Christ made these things when he was a child. When he was just Jesu, her beloved youngest brother.

He was not beloved by her, not for a long time. How could he be, considering he was the favourite of their father, who had the boy when he was an old man? They were never like brother and sister and she had enough brothers to know what a real brother was like. Jesus was no brother. He was the spoilt one carried like a precious gemstone by his mother, who was the same age as she. Her father loved him with an old man's unfaltering love. But Joseph was her father before he became father to Jesus. Why did he need to be reminded of this?

It is early in the day and already hot and she wants to go home. She has had nothing to eat but a crust of bread and goat's milk. Sometimes she goes for most of a day without customers. But she is sitting in the sparse shade of the old gates and selling stories out of a blanket. She thinks herself lucky that she is not like her brothers who work the land for a pittance, their hands calloused like the bark of a tree. Or she could be like Lydia. Confined to a room in her brother's house and talking to dust motes, weeping at the dusk, enraged by a leaf. The last time she went to visit, her sweet sister had smeared her monthly blood on the walls of her room. They spoke through a barred window. Her sister was shaking with anger.

'Let me out,' she said. 'I didn't do it. You know me. I would never murder a child. The real murderer is out there – there.'

Then her mood changed swiftly and completely. She fitted her soiled hands through the bars and said:

'Sister, don't you want to play with me?'

It is the time of day when her thoughts boil like soup. The sun is directly above and it beats on her head with a metallic sound. She notes that the thoroughfare out of the city is choked with dust and the water carrier has not wet the roads today. A man walks past with a mule and sends up a small yellow cloud. The dust is a living thing that saps her interest and makes her feel old. She will pack up and go home. But the man who has been watching her saunters up to ask about the donkey figure placed at the centre of

139

the blanket. His hands are not the hands of a working man and his beard is trimmed and shaped with oil. He picks up the donkey and examines it.

'Is this the beast on which he rode to Jerusalem? Or is it the one his mother rode when she was pregnant and wandering the countryside?'

She cannot think this noon. Her brain cooks in the pan of her skull and fish shapes swim around the edges of her vision. What is Lydia doing at this moment, what kind of bliss or rage is she enacting? For a moment she envies her lovely sister who is lost in her own head and happy to let her imaginings create the world. What would she make of this man whose smooth face and cold eyes show not a glimmer of hope? She should have listened when they were children. She should have talked more to Jesus.

'You must have some stories you don't tell, am I right?' the man says.

'No,' she says.

'No stories about your brother you haven't told anyone?' The man smiles and two clefts appear in his smooth cheeks. Then the smile vanishes as if he has just recalled something unpleasant.

When she doesn't reply the man says, 'How many years do you have?' She shakes her head. 'You don't enjoy talking much,' he says. 'That's good. Everyone should have secrets, even the sister of the Christ.'

The man strokes the donkey with both hands. He is wearing a gold ring on his thumb. His hands are bony but the nails are tended and the skin appears soft to the touch. He says, 'Your brother must have told you things he didn't tell anyone else?'

She tells the man that her brother was the youngest of the family and a born storyteller, but only if he was in the mood. Most often he watched silently and made notes in his head for fables he would deliver in the future. He was always good that way, she says. He had the voice and the imagination and he could make up fantastic tales at will. It was a gift. The timeless arrow-like stories that would make birds alight from the trees and the lion mew like a helpless kitten. The man fixes his eye on her and grips the tiny head and twists and the donkey falls in pieces to the ground. Straw spills to the blanket. Somehow she has made him angry by delivering a speech she has made countless times to customers. He examines her body as if it too is for sale.

'I imagine you nailed to a tilted cross, your legs spread and nailed,' he says. 'I don't imagine you lasting very long.'

She gets to her feet. She is an old widow woman with shaky knees.

'Do you know who I am?' he says.

'Yes. I know you.'

'Then you know I'll be back and if I see you here, you will suffer like your brother. Try and remember what happened to him.'

'I know you and I've always known you,' she says. 'You are a brown crow who preys on poor women.'

She spits near his feet.

The man smiles then and displays small teeth widely spaced in fleshy black gums. He nods and walks away. It is another day in the life of a woman whose brother died on the cross.

Her name is Assia, the sister of Lydia and of Jesus.

# 19

They stopped cleaning the walls and the floor because they cannot bear to touch her blood. They think she does not notice but she does, of course she does. She sees everything. The fear on the faces of her brothers when they bring her food. The lack of fear on the face of her father's new wife when she comes to visit, which is rarely. The absence of the father she has not seen since she was a child. Of all the absences of her life, this is the one she wants to undo. Her father would know how to make his sons see the truth. He would know to fix her. She dips into herself and creates a face that is her father's exactly, down to the sunken eyes and the soft white beard that hangs to his chest. The passage of the weeks and months she has been in this room are inscribed for all to see in layers of red, the early layers turning now into ochre streaked by lumps of coagulate and clot, the tissue of which she is the mistress, the living tissue that is available to her only, measured in months. The texture of red marks the gradation of colour from within, and the ridges and valleys and faces on the wall populate her nightmares and dreams. But only one of the faces she has created from the well inside her is more than just colour. Her sweet old father. Looking into his face makes her happy.

How is she so happy so suddenly? How is she so fresh when she has not slept a wink? Her night was not night but set upon by a whiteness that seemed to come from the moon. It seeped in from the window and crossed the floor and slipped easily into her ears. She tried to change positions and sleep with her head at the foot of the bed but the light found her. Towards morning she dreamed of her sister, though it took a long time for her to understand that it was Assia and she was locked in a house guarded by soldiers, and the soldiers were not Romans but Jews. She knew they were Jews even if they were dressed as Romans, even if they had hidden all outward sign of their faith and high status. Her sister's captors were Jews disguised as Romans and when she tried to communicate this to her sister, Assia covered her ears. No, she kept saying. No, you're wrong. I'm not being kept against my will. I can leave whenever I want.

Going to the window she moves the dirty curtain with her red hands. She hears the wind breaking like surf against the trees, the sunlight breaking in waves against the ground, the sky saturated with white, obscuring the crowns of the trees and the air itself. In those slow hours she feels herself become a sentinel of the long trees, guardian of the white light that drips in waves towards the houses around her. She is become a watcher. But in the field outside are the true watchers. Her brothers do not believe her when she tries to tell them. Somehow when they look there is no one in the field. She warns them but they will not listen. When the world ends they will be in the first rank, she knows, waving and begging to be taken. Or they will try to take shelter behind their shadows and the shadows of their children. They will have forgotten by then that each man is nailed to his own shadow as to the bloody cross. The thought of her brothers' fate adds a shiver of excitement to her happiness. This is the way it must be, she says to herself. Energised, she cups her hands around her mouth and screams at the watcher who is closest, a thin youth wrapped in a horse blanket.

'Come here,' she shouts, in a voice she is unable to recognise as hers or her father's. A voice that does not sound like anyone she knows. 'Come and try me, if you're so brave.'

To the old God and the new I ask the same question, she says to the faces on the wall. Who waits near the juniper at my window? Is it the same thief who holds me to the light? Why does he wish for my death? Does he not know this is what I wish for myself?

She hears a voice and she searches among the faces until she finds the one that pretends it has not spoken. But she knows it is her youngest brother, whom she has not seen since they were children. Or she has seen him once, when he came to the house of his parents and his brothers seized him and held him before the crowd that had gathered. She and Assia stayed in the house. Her sister managed to stay calm. She did not. Her agitation was so intense she felt it in her stomach like a blow. She wanted her brothers to let him go. Or at least they should not have held him so roughly. Anyone could see he had no will to leave. He stood limp in their arms while his brothers heaped infamy on his head.

'He is insane,' said Joses, holding him by the neck. 'He has taken leave of his senses. It's clear to see.'

'No,' said Simon, who had hold of his arms. 'It is worse even than that. He is possessed by the Devil and by Beelzebub. Both. At the same time.'

Jesus said something she could not hear, such was the hubbub around him. He spoke in his low voice even while addressing the multitude. She moved closer and heard him say that the prophet was without honour in his own house. The prophet was lauded by all, except his own family, his own brothers and sisters. Shamed, she went into the crowd. Assia tried to stop her but she pulled free and shouted at her brothers to let him go. Here was her youngest brother who had left home and never returned, and when finally he did return, to be greeted in such a way. They ignored her, which made her angry. Then Joses, Jude and Simon took him to the outskirts of Nazareth. The crowd followed, excited to see what they would do with him. They were disappointed when the brothers let him go and told him not to return. He had no home in Nazareth now that he had declared himself a leader and rebel and enemy of the Jews. He had divided their house and it was only correct, then, that he no longer had a house.

There were two immediate results of the humiliation that his brothers visited upon Jesus. It seemed that many among the Jews sympathised with him. Others, who wished an end to the rule of the Romans, saw in him the leader they had waited for. When it became clear that only the high priests and elders of the temple were opposed to him, her brothers had a change of heart. Or they pretended to have a change of heart. When they went to him with Assia and his mother, he would not meet them. This was the first result of her brothers' actions. The second was more humiliating for the family. She, the youngest of their sisters, the bright one whose light would shine furthest and longest, she it was who lost her senses and fell insane. She was seized by Beelzebub. Soon after their return from the failed attempt to see Jesus, she was subject to the first of her screaming visitations. When they became more frequent her brothers confined her to a room in the old house where she remains, having lost count of the days and months, knowing only that there are too many.

As she gazes at his face the lips begin to move and she hears the voice of her youngest brother. The soft and halting speech that sounds as if it is unsure of itself and doubts its own existence. This, she knows, is the quality that brings the followers to him in throngs and makes it impossible for his family to get close to him. The quality of doubt. This is what makes his followers love him. The shyness that sits oddly and comfortably with his great ambition and his old hunger to communicate with as many people as possible, Jew or Gentile, fisherman or carpenter or spy, criminal or priest.

The mouth moves imperceptibly. The voice is faltering and smooth. The man hidden by the juniper outside the window was sent by the temple elders to create divisions amongst you, says the voice, to sow them as he sows seeds for the harvest. He is here to take you to the temple, so the people may see you as the sister of the man who calls himself King of the Jews. If the people see that you are insane they will see your brother for the liar that he is. As to the old God and the new, they are one and the same.

You may address to me your question to him. I may or may not be the King of the Jews (and if I am, so is every man), but certainly I can answer a question put to God (as can you). The man who hides by the juniper is not the same one who shines the light that finds your face. That light is a direct line from heaven. A silver reminder that you are seen and you are cherished. You have been touched. Touched, she says to the red face. Did you say touched? I know where I've been touched. In the head, isn't that right? If you are worried that you are touched in the head, then you are not. But why should I believe you? she asks. Because I am your brother and I have never lied, not to you. And now let me answer your last question, as to why the man wishes for your death and whether he knows this is what you wish for yourself. He does not and he does not. And neither do you. What you wish for is a sense of calm, perhaps even a luxuriant boredom. Is wishing for calm and boredom the same as wishing to die? No, it is not. It is the opposite, a desire to live and the longing for a small breeze against your face, or moonlight in your window, or birdsong in the morning.

Moonlight? she says to herself, rushing to the window to part the curtains. The watchers are gone. The sandstone houses next to the houses of her brothers are still and quiet. The juniper leans slightly into the sun. Its bottom half is denuded. The leaves are lit from within, as if by raw honey. Broken light waves between the branches like yellow clouds on a morning when the air is no longer a barrier between this world and the next, but an invitation and a covenant. The open doorway that welcomes, rather than a dirty curtain that separates.

Yes, moonlight, says the face on the wall. Its lips move into an obscure smile reminiscent of the oracle of Delphi, if the oracle was given to smiling. Without it, sunlight would not mark a new day and its light would be lost light. In the same way, says the face, without me the history of Israel is lost. My history is the history of the nation. If this is true of me, it is true of everyone. For instance, he tells her, I was born in Bethlehem but as far as the populace is concerned I am from Nazareth in Galilee. Have you ever wondered why this is so? I have not, she says, smiling. There are many things I wonder about but this is not one of them. Forgive me. Why is it so? she asks. Because when I was born the Idumean Herod ordered Bethlehem's male children to be killed. Did you know that much at least? I think I did, she says. He ordered that all male children under the age of two should be drowned or strangled or placed on the tip of a sword. So my father, who is also yours, fled to Egypt with my mother and me. Years later, when we returned, our father preferred to be cautious, lest word spread that I had survived the Idumean's edict and come back to Israel. Instead of returning to Bethlehem or going to Jerusalem, our father chose Galilee, a small and unknown town where we could live without fear. So that's why he disappeared for such a long time, she says. Do you wonder why it is that your brothers and sisters resent you? It is because we were abandoned because of you and we are unable to forgive you. Yes, says the face, I know, and I say it is time to forgive the infant I was. I was too young. I knew little of death. I didn't understand that it is only a marker on the road. It is not the road's end. A marker, she says. Is that what you have come to tell me? Yes, sister of

148

my childhood. I have come to tell you nothing more than this. That the events to which you are beholden are only markers. The children you beget and the wealth you beget and the children you lose and the wealth you lose, the good health you enjoy and the illness you rue, all of it – nothing more than markers for you who are lost on the road.

Her name is Lydia, sister of Assia and of Jesus.

# 20

The moment they gain the road to Jerusalem the rain begins, small drops that darken the dust. She puts her cloak over her son and they huddle under the donkey. A whisper of locusts rises from the ground and a smell of earth and rot. Immediately she is soaked through. The landscape dissolves before her eyes, flattened by the downpour.

'On top of everything,' she says. 'Just when I can't take another step. Can we wait here until it stops?'

'Yes, why not?' says her husband. 'Give them time to catch us and string us up. They won't care about taking us alive, do you know that?'

'In this kind of rain, who knows anything,' she says sweetly. 'I barely remember my name.'

'We'll be safe once we find my friend.'

Small rivulets form around her sandals. The rain is so heavy she cannot see the churning of the ground. Her husband takes the rope of the donkey while she holds her infant son and tries not to lose her footing. She longs for a dry bed at the inn they will not see again. The fixed daily rounds, the meals she cooked and rooms she cleaned, the animals they fed and watered, even the chores she disliked now seem like a blessing. She holds her son to her chest and wonders at his sweet nature. How is it that he isn't crying? She says her husband's name and then her own, but she cannot be heard over the sound of the rain. How quickly the old life came to an end! All it took was a day.

The old man arrived soon after nightfall. His animals were overladen and his slaves carried so many bundles it was surprising he had managed to evade the bandits on the road. He hadn't been prepared for bandits of another kind. Didn't he know that in the wilderness between Jericho and Jerusalem no authority prevailed except the ancient authority of bludgeon and murder? In these parts thieves set the law and answered to no man or king. And it was the thief's law to which she and her husband owed allegiance. She noticed that one of the old man's slaves carried two daggers. There were ritual piercings in his ears, which meant he had been freed and had chosen to stay with his master. She had never before seen a freed slave. The slave liked to laugh and he enjoyed his drink. But the old man, his master, looked sickly. He had suffered from the journey and his skin was shiny with sweat. He kept clearing his throat. It sounded to her like the grunts of a dying animal.

When he asked for food she served them roasted meat with a loaf she had baked that morning and some bowls of oil. The slave who liked to laugh ate enough for two men and fell asleep on the table. At the end of his meal the old man asked for honey and new wine. Coughing, he drank. It gave him comfort for a time but soon he was back to clearing his throat. The grating filled her ears. It reminded her of a cypress tree being stripped of its bark. After she cleared the dishes she showed him to the best room and put his slaves in the small cell at the back of the house, as far from their master as possible. Then she went outside to tell her husband that the old man was sick, a cougher, and he would be alone for the night. His slaves had drunk too much of the strong wine. Soon they would be asleep.

They waited until the moon was high before entering his room. He came awake at once. Her husband had to hold him down while she searched his bags. His struggles were fierce for a sick old man. He pushed himself out of the bed and shouted, Oh, oh, so loudly they must have heard at the other side of the house. He kicked over the night table and the candle stand crashed to the ground. Just when they thought he had given up he tore her husband's cheek with his nails. They twisted around each other like cats. By then she wanted him dead. Kill, she hissed to her husband. Kill! What are you waiting for? Her husband put his forearm across the old man's throat and pushed hard. They heard a muffled snap and the man's eyes came fully open, which made her husband push harder. They heard another snap, though not as loud as the first. The old man clawed for her husband's face and could not reach it. His bladder emptied as he died. All that marked his passing was the sharp smell of urine. She waited. Her breath heaved as she listened for sounds in the house. Then she opened his robe and found a folded blue cloth tied around his midriff. In it, thumb-sized lumps of gold and some finger-rings and a pouch of silver coin. She was trying on one of the rings when they saw the freed slave with the pierced ears and twin daggers. He was struggling to speak.

'My master, Hiram?'

'Hiram?'

'My master.'

'Hiram, the tax collector?'

'Yes.'

'Friend to the high-born and protector of the wealthy?'

'Yes, yes!'

The young slave fell to his knees. He forgot he was speaking to his master's killers. He forgot he was in possession of two daggers. He forgot everything except that Hiram was dead and he had no master. Behind him the two other slaves huddled at the door, their frightened eyes large in the firelight. What were they waiting for? Why did they not attack their master's killers? They stared at each other. When her husband reached for his knife, the men moved quickly out of the room and bolted the door from the outside. It took her husband little time to kick his way through but by then the three had vanished. They would return with others. She and her husband would be arrested and executed. They would have to hurry, if they wished to live.

She packed bread and oil in a cloth bundle and linen in another. Her husband took whatever weapons he could find. They left everything, the rooms as they had always been, ready for guests, the plates in need of washing, the unmade beds, the chairs and tables they had fashioned themselves, the candles still burning on the sill. They left the old life. They took only the gold and silver and some provisions and the donkey.

Her son laughs and gurgles on her hip as if he understands everything that has brought them here, climbing a mountain on their great adventure. There are spit bubbles on his chin. He smiles at her and shakes his head and dimples his plump cheeks. As they ascend into the mountains the rain thins into mist. A wet hanging vapour adheres to their cloaks. The sky is so dark it seems night has already fallen. She has never been so far into the mountains. She knows only that it is a place of outcasts. The solitary and insane men and women spurned by all others. Those revolutionaries or traitors who are hunted by the authorities. There is no vegetation but for the occasional stunted tree with short branches at the top. But at least the rain has stopped. Steam rises in clouds from the sodden ground and far above she hears the wheeling cry of a hawk.

When they stop to eat a crust of bread she gives the sleeping baby to her husband. There are no other travellers to be seen but she goes behind a rock out of habit. She gathers her tunic around her waist and has just begun to relieve herself when she sees a bundled shape hanging from a tree. It is the body of a woman strung upside down and bled dry. She does not scream but calmly continues. The dead woman is young. The skin on her face has set like swollen dark porridge. Blood has run along her hairline and congealed in a pool on the ground. She calls her husband, who only nods and tells her to hurry. Further up the mountain they find the corpse of a portly middle-aged man displayed in the same fashion, upside down, the blood drained from a single cut to the throat as if in observance of the rules of ritual slaughter. Her husband says:

154

'This is Gestas.'

'Your friend?'

'This is him. I'd know his work anywhere.'

'What do you mean, his work? Blood is blood.'

'No, it really isn't. See how clean the cut is, no shredding or sawing, just precision.'

'Your friend, the careful butcher.'

'We're getting close now. Come on.'

He leads the donkey with one hand, the other holding the baby to his chest. She picks her way carefully among the rocks. This high, the drop is sheer all the way down to the plains. There are loose rocks and boulders. Her husband takes a sharp bend in the path and she loses sight of him. Instantly a large hand is clamped across her mouth. She is pulled to the ground and a knife is at her throat. She does not struggle. Her husband returns and finds her on the ground, her hair twisted in her captor's hand. He puts his knife away and settles the baby on his hip. There is a broad smile on his face as he embraces the man, who is brushing dirt from his clothes. Her husband says, This is Gestas, my friend and colleague. They return the way they came and, behind a screen of thorny bush and cut branches, there is the entrance to a cave.

She sees meat cooking on a spit and salted fish spread to dry on a ledge. She sees chewed bones on the ground and discarded apple cores. She sees a short man, round but not fat, with a fleshy face and small cunning eyes. The cave stinks of old food and old sweat and fish. The man Gestas drinks wine from a large skin. He won't share. He speaks quietly with long pauses, as if he is saying something important and must think it through carefully. But he isn't saying anything important. He is saying something foolish.

'Now, there's a noise no one has heard on this mountain for a long time. A baby. I am not a devotee of children. There aren't any on my mountain, as you may have noticed. My kingdom is childless and so it will remain.'

'Your mountain? Your kingdom?'

'Mine. I'm the King here.'

'King,' she says, her voice full of amusement. 'King of what? A cave and some meat?'

'Be careful. I might need a fresh marker for the road and you'd do nicely for today.'

Her husband laughs and tells them both to settle down.

Gestas says: 'This is your wife? Where did you steal her from? Can't you find a way to govern her tongue?'

'There is no way to govern her,' says her husband. 'The women of her family are all the same. They are impossible to govern.'

After he has eaten, Gestas climbs on the ledge where salted meat and fish have been laid out to dry. She asks him about the bodies.

'To dissuade others from coming up,' he says.

'Didn't dissuade us,' says her husband.

'Call it a display. Keeps people away and brings them to me also. That is the main reason they are hanging from the trees. Think of it as a sign for those who know and for those who are looking. Isn't that how you found me, Dismas? You knew to follow the bodies.'

'Some kind of royalty,' she says. 'The insane king of the mountain.'

He stares at her and the infant on her breast. He takes a deep drink and slaps his thigh. He addresses only her:

'The people who come here are similar in one way. They want to die. All of them want to die. When I kill them, I am carrying out their wishes. I am a merciful man and I do it quickly, without much pain. Then I bleed them so they won't rot too soon and I honour them by putting up their bodies for other travellers to see.'

The baby gurgles happily and holds out his hand to Gestas.

'What's his name?'

'We haven't named him yet.'

The baby laughs.

'I like him,' Gestas says. 'He's a good boy.'

'Yes, he is,' she says, taking her son to him. The boy reaches for Gestas's scar. A smile spreads across his plump face.

'Still doesn't mean I want babies on my mountain,' Gestas says. 'You know, sometimes I stop to say a few words to the hanging ones. I might say, how is it now, young lady, where you are? Isn't it an improvement? She never answers but she agrees, you can see it on her face. I cut them the correct way with a small curved blade. One cut from ear to ear. The important thing is, don't stop, don't falter, don't hesitate. When you draw your knife, use it. Cut with one cut. Shlomo. Did you see their faces?'

'Of course we saw their faces.'

'No, but did you look carefully? Go and look. There are more as you go higher up the mountain. Look at their faces and tell me what you see. Tell me if there is any trace of fear. There is not, because at the last moment they know they are in the hands of God's butcher. They love me because they know I kill them tenderly and thoughtfully. I love God in the same way. He has killed so many. He is skilled at killing. How can we not love the master who kills us well?'

He makes himself comfortable on the ledge and takes another deep drink from the wineskin. The baby holds out his hands.

'We'll leave tomorrow,' her husband says. 'We want to reach Jerusalem quickly. Our pursuers aren't far behind. If they catch us they'll take us back to Jericho and imprison us, or worse.'

'Let them come. On the mountain all men and women are equal. Maybe women are more equal,' says Gestas dreamily.

Then he speaks about the people who come to his mountain, how strange they are, so strange that even he, Gestas, whose mountain they have trespassed on, even he lets them alone. If he doesn't kill them first. He tells them about a young man who made his dwelling in a cave on the first slope. A man dressed in nothing, who lived on insects and the food people left for him. He stayed for years and never ventured far past the mouth of the cave.

'I met him only once. He liked to stand on one leg wearing a blanket made from the moth-eaten skin of a camel or a donkey. That was all he wore, whatever the weather. I asked him why he didn't stand on two legs like other men. Do you know what he said?'

'I'm sure I don't,' she says.

'He said, "I am the door. Anyone may enter through me." So I said, "A door? To what exactly?" He laughed in a way that split his hairy face in two and at that moment

158

his mouth did seem to me like a door into another world. He said, "I am the door, enter and be saved." Well, I chose not to enter, though maybe I should have. To tell you the truth, he troubled me. I didn't want to meet him again.'

'Why didn't you make a marker out of him, like you did with the others? Why did you let him live?'

'I got the feeling he didn't want to die just yet. I still think about him from time to time, the man who stood on one leg. Sometimes I talk to him.'

'You talk to him. But what does he say?'

'He talks of an uprising. He says if we rise up together against those who call themselves our priests, then it isn't revolution but self-knowledge. If you force your tongue to listen rather than speak, it will bring to life that which will save you. If you do not bring it to life, it will cause the illness that will destroy you. These are the things he tells me.'

Saying this, Gestas puts the wineskin under his head and stretches out on the ledge and falls asleep to loud snores.

'I've seen him,' says her husband. 'The man Gestas was talking about. I heard him talk about the priests and I agree. They are swine. If you want to be a thief you should be honest.'

Soon her husband too is snoring. With the baby in her arms and her husband's knife under her hip, she falls into a light sleep and dreams of priests and murder.

All the next day they rest. They repair their sandals, water and rub down the donkey, pack salted meat and nuts. When night falls they take to the mountain road by the light of a half-moon. On their way down the steep sides of the unnamed mountain, the lost domain of Gestas, they pass the dwelling of the man he told them about. The disturbed man who stood on one leg and invited people to enter through him into another world. What kind of world? And what if return was impossible? Travellers have left a collection of objects at the mouth of the cave, as if it was once the abode of a saint. Dried flowers, rotten figs, empty casks, some lengths of torn linen. The moonlight turns everything into silver talismans, harbingers of good luck or bad, lost objects they do not wish to touch.

They travel through the night and enter the great gates of Jerusalem just after dawn. Near a synagogue she stops to wash her son and change his swaddling clothes. She puts on a clean robe and washes the red dust from her face. She is tidying her hair when she hears a commotion from the entrance to the synagogue.

She sees the man she calls her husband dragged along the street. His hands are restrained by a small crowd of men. He is made to stand in the road while the priests ask him one question after the other. Who is he? Why has he come? Does he know the punishment for defiling the synagogue? No mercy will be shown him. Does he know? The objects he tried to steal, did he not care that they were sacred? What kind of a thief would steal from the house of God? The high priest displays to the crowd a menorah made of gold. When they take him away to a place called Golgotha, the place of skulls, according to the men who are his captors, he passes so close she might have kissed him. He shakes his head very slightly and acts as if he does not know her. She lets him pass.

Her name is Shoshamma, wife of Dismas, the penitent thief.

# 21

It's always in the head that the voice makes itself heard, never in the chest or the belly or the hands. The head is the culprit, she thinks. Thoughts originate there. No wonder they behead you. No wonder they hang you and crucify you with a crown of thorns and impale you by the neck on a spike. It's all to silence the head. And what does the voice say? Always the same two words. *Am I?* Over and over, first thing in the morning and last thing at night. Until the words mean more than their meaning. Until they are the sound of the sun setting and the sound of the moon when the sky is black. *Am I Am I Am I?* Until it becomes the opposite: *I Am I Am I Am.* When repeated long enough, she understands at last, a question answers itself.

Word comes to the village of the man who dresses in camel's hair. A prophet whose meat is locusts and honey. Assia has no idea what it means – she hears, locusts *in* honey and imagines a kind of wild delicacy – but she wants to see him.

'He throws you in the river,' Assia says. 'He throws you in and holds you under. You think you're drowning but then he pulls you up.'

'And this sounds like fun to you?' Lydia asks. 'A pleasant way to spend the afternoon?'

'He's my cousin – I mean *our* cousin. I want to see for myself what the excitement is about. Don't you?'

She doesn't, but she cannot let her sister go alone.

'I don't know,' she says. 'I have enough excitement as it is. I could do with a little less of it in my life.'

'Oh, Lydia, your voices again?'

'What do you mean, again? They didn't go anywhere, they're always here,' she says, jabbing at her temple with a forefinger.

They leave without telling any of their brothers except Simon, who insists on coming. They would have liked to tell Jesus, but he is never at home. They haven't seen him in months. He is already a name or an echo, the storyteller about whom stories are told, the figure seen in multiple places at once. To her, he is a stranger who visits while on his way somewhere else. Usually he is accompanied by the unkempt men who look past her and her family, who do not speak and do not listen and respond only to the man they call the Christ. By then he is already saying the things that gather to his side the lost and sickly and insane. He knows what ails a man or a woman simply by looking at them. He will lay a hand on the head or heart or liver and say: Here, this is where the pain is. But he won't do anything about it. He won't heal. That comes later.

When they reach the river they find a crowd. Travellers selling sides of meat and flagons of goat's milk, a man carrying a falcon in a cage, another selling hand-drums, as if it is a feast day, which it is not. They make their way slowly through the mass of people. She hears the words of

162

the song the crowd is singing carried to her on the wind from the water, a song she has never before heard. It sounds cheerful but the cheer is false. Inside, the song is so sad it will never be happy again. Near the sandy bank they catch a glimpse of water and hundreds of men and women and children facing the same way. The ground is wet mud and her sandals are immediately sucked in and ruined. She wants to turn back. The crowd stops singing as a head breaks the water and a man emerges, dripping.

The Baptist, her cousin John, is young and his thick hair is already streaked with white. She remembers him as a smiling young man who liked to fight. His knuckles were always scratched and raw-looking. Green veins snaked in a tangle on the backs of his hands. But he had a smiling word for all those he met and he was well liked. Now he is a gaunt forbidding figure who does not smile, whose long beard sprouts from his chin like waterweeds. He speaks in a tongue she cannot decipher. What is he saying? The wild-looking man knee-deep in the river forces a terrified child into the water and holds him under while the crowd chants his name. With a powerful hand at his head, the Baptist pulls the boy out – the child snorting for air, black water streaming from his hair and nose – and tosses him to willing hands that bring him to shore and leave him prone in the mud, where he wets himself. He screams for his mother, who is in the river waiting her turn.

A group of old men kneel in the shallows, their hands raised to the sky. 'Take me,' they shout. 'No, take me.' One of them tears his tunic into pieces and rips the cloth from his torso. Nails rake across the bony sunken chest. Faint red lines take shape on the ribs. 'Take me,' he shouts. 'Praise, Baptist!'

Her cousin ignores the old men. His rough face is tilted to heaven and he is singing in the most beautiful voice she has ever heard. The cadence and melody are known to her and though the language sounds familiar, she is unable to understand the meaning. Is it the tongue of a neighbouring country, or a language spoken by children, or did the Baptist make it up on his travels? Some parts of the song are so intensely familiar, but just as her understanding alights on a word, it dances away.

Simon dares her to go into the river.

'Can't hurt,' he says. 'What are you waiting for?'

Assia joins in: 'Do it, Lydia, go on. He is only our cousin, our John, why are you afraid? It's nothing more than a bath in the river. I know you've been thinking about it.'

No, no. She is not thinking about anything except her swollen feet. She is still young but she can feel her body grow old, weighing her mind with strange dreams and unruly thoughts. The crowd is too much for her. The look in their eyes is too much. They are waiting to see her naked, to ridicule her old woman's body though she is not old. She will not expose herself to them. Baptism, it seems to her, is taking off your clothes in front of a crowd of rowdy strangers and inviting their opinion about your hips and face and belly. They are not interested in a baptism. What they really want is to see her dead body in the water. She will not do it. She takes Assia's hand and pulls her away and Simon reluctantly follows.

For days afterwards she hears his voice crying out in the familiar unfamiliar language. At times she understands perfectly the hoarse warnings that God's wrath is nigh, that his wrath is steadfast and will not be diverted, that

164

the same fate befalls the foolish as the wicked. Moral stupidity is as grave a sin as moral blindness and why should it not be punished? Between the promises of brimstone she hears the familiar words. *I am.* She hears the proclamation. There is one coming who will heal the wounds of their sins, the thousand and one cuts of greed, the open sores of fornication. He, John, is only a messenger for the prophet who is already on his way to lift the blight that has descended on the land. She does not know, then, that the Baptist is talking about her own youngest brother, Jesus, who is half a brother, with whom she shares a father and no mother.

Late that first night after the visit to the river she dreams of bullfrogs that cover a field in which she is buried. In the rich loamy soil she hears the songs of the worms that wish to befriend her, in the language she knows but cannot recognise, though she has no trouble understanding the words. God's anger is infinite, they sing. His jokes are infinite too, but harder to follow. She wonders if this is a joke against her, to fill the world with tongues that sound familiar but remain always on the verge of comprehension.

She sleeps late and wakes early, unable to breathe. She is constricted by the walls of her room and the narrow bed like a coffin in which she must lie on her back. There are voices nearby and one among them is the voice that awakened her. The soft and inhuman tones of her youngest brother. Is she imagining this too? Or is it the voice of the Baptist and she cannot tell the difference? But when she steps out of her room she finds her brother, and the family gathered around him. For once he is alone. He tells them he is on his way to the river to see the Baptist John.

'We went,' says Assia. 'Yesterday. We even considered baptism, at least Lydia did, but at the last moment she couldn't go through with it. Why are you going?'

'I want a fresh dip in the river. I could use a nice bath.'

For a moment no one says anything. Then they understand that their serious young brother has made a joke and they laugh too loudly. Another silence follows and this is when she asks if she may go with him.

In truth it was not baptism that he sought. He must have known from the start that he would be recognised. Could it be that he went to the river for this reason, to be recognised? Why else would he greet his cousin with an argument as to who was the greater prophet? As if they were still boys playing games in the field. It's you! No, no, it is you! But seriously, it's you! She notices how similar they are and how similarly stubborn. Both refuse to budge, adamant in the positions they have taken. They even look alike, she thinks. Some emanation in the face that creates a mystery around the things they say. Some quality that puts a distance in the eyes, as if they are looking so far into the future they cannot see those who are standing in front of them. Her brother's clothes are finer and his beard has been recently shaped. His skin is oiled. He isn't as weather-beaten. But otherwise they are so similar they could be reflections. The argument goes on until John holds up his hands and says:

'I am the messenger and you are the message. How will the messenger baptise the message?'

'Cousin, this message has been on the road for many a long day. It needs a nice bath.'

166

The people around them laugh at the old joke. Only the Baptist does not.

'Baptise me, cousin,' says her brother.

'How can I, when I know who you are?'

Her brother's breathing slows. When he speaks it is in a whisper:

'You are John the Baptist. I am here today not as your childhood friend but as a man. Baptise me!'

She hears a new voice then, more inhuman than the voice of her brother and softer too. The dizziness comes on her and she closes her eyes but the voice only gets louder. A rain of white water falls around her. When she opens her eyes, she is on the ground and there is a strange taste in her mouth. Hands lift her, tender hands that remind her of her mother who left her when she was still a small child. Left her and died, the worst way to leave someone. The hands that lift her belong to those who heard her speak in another tongue, as one possessed by God. Someone immerses her in the river, she does not know who, her brother or her cousin or strangers. She comes up streaming water and saying his name. *Jesu*.

'Gone,' says the Baptist. 'Slipped away while you were in the water.'

'But where?'

'He said a wilderness, the mountains, the desert, somewhere without men or women, there to think and be with the beasts and God.'

She knows she will never see him again.

Lydia, sister to James, Joses, Judas, Simon, Assia and Jesus.

# 22

Imagine the savour and the disappointment as I sailed above the earth and looked down from my wooden mast. I saw the war to come, the sacking of Jerusalem, the soldiers marching into the temple to gird with steel the Ark of the Covenant, the temple set afire to burn into the night and half the day, and the hunger among the people, mothers taking any morsel of food from the mouths of their infants, and the plunder, the rape of the city, every man, woman and child put to the sword, their heads torn and adorned on spikes, bodies spread, tied against the pillars or left to rot in the streets. All this I saw. Then I returned to the hill whose name was my death. At my feet my mother and you, but neither of my sisters nor one of my father's four sons, those men who are not my brothers or half my brothers until it behoves them to be. And so I gave this John to my mother, because the son of her blood would soon be gone and the others had run away. I told her, behold thy son! I saw who I am. And who am I if I am not Dismas, the penitent robber to the left of me, or Gestas the impenitent to my right? And I in the middle, worse than any thief, for I am nailed while they are only tied.

The son of man need only be tied but he who is the Son of God and of man, what punishment equals his crime? For saying to you that the Christ is you and the family you find is truer than the one you are born into. This is the family of you multiplied a hundred times. There among you are the twelve men to replace the leaders of the twelve tribes. There among you twelve hundred men and women, each the Christ. The others will say they come in my name or in the name of the Father, but the only name they honour is their own. They will say the kingdom is in heaven only. Train your ear. He who says the kingdom is around you and within you, only he honours you. Train your eye. The day is here that burns as fire. The buildings they have raised and worshipped as unto God, the cities, the paper, the images, all will float upon the firmament and sink. These last I offer you, Mary, secret words that you, my twin, may make whole and put into the world, so each man and woman may also be my twin, identical to me, more than Christians: Christs.

# 23

At the end of her life she remembered not the death of her son but the first days of her fullness. She was betrothed to an old man who lived far away and she was with child – a child with child. She had become the girl who was given away. Three years of age when her old mother gave her to a priest at the temple, twelve when the priest gave her to a man so old she was younger than his children. Why was she given away, and given away? They said it was because she had been promised to God. But God could not keep her. He too sent her away once the monthly blood was upon her. The impurity that began and stopped. This is what they said and she knew otherwise. They gave her away because she was unwanted. It makes her wonder, how long before she is given away again?

She has grown up a child of the temple, a source of amusement to the priests and those who come to worship. The strange child who knows the scripture and corrects the priests, but knows no children's games or songs and is serious beyond her years and never seems to laugh. The child who does not know to be childish. By the age of eight her memories of her parents are uncertain. She remembers an old woman and the name Anna and she remembers being hungry. She knows nothing of how she came to the temple except the stories she has been told. That she was unnaturally quiet. That her parents were old enough to be her grandparents and when they left her with the priest, she did not cry or look back but walked up the steps and into the doors of her new home.

Her clearest memory is dismay. She was sure her parents would return. The reason she did not look back was because she did not know she was being given away. Her mother didn't tell her. It was only later that she understood they were gone. For days afterwards, for months, she expected them to return. She waited to be taken home. But her mother did not come and she knew it was her own fault. If she had been a boy, would her mother have sent her away? Never. Her mother and her father would have loved her and kept her.

Another story they tell her is that her parents were so old they did not expect to have children. Her mother had given herself up to childlessness. She said to her husband that there were worse things in the world. Then, one day when she was already an old woman, Anna saw a birds' nest. She saw the baby birds fed by the mother. She saw how wide the babies opened their mouths and how patiently the mother fed each one and she wanted her own nest. She prayed and her husband prayed. She made a promise to God. If she were blessed with a child she would dedicate him to the temple. When the priest got to this part of the story she always interrupted him. Why did Anna pray for a child if she was going to give me away? And the priest would look at her as if she were no longer a child but a troublesome petitioner. He had no answer. The look in his eyes was unreadable and she knew. He too would give her away. He didn't want her.

'I won't ask any more questions,' she said, frightened.

'You will ask what you want,' said the priest.

'I better not,' she said.

'This is God's house. You can always ask. Answers are another matter. God is not always forthcoming with his answers.'

The priest laughed at his joke. It was a quiet laugh that sounded like he was coughing. He stopped when he saw the girl's expression. But it was already too late. By then they had decided what they would do with her. She knew this. It was only a matter of time. Some weeks later the head priest takes her for a walk in the courtyard. She has come to think of him as her father. He tells her there are important men coming to the temple to see her and she must look her best. He does not say why they are coming.

In the morning she goes to the well to collect water and finds the women gathered, taking their time as if it is a feast day. They fall silent when they see her. At the temple she bathes and puts oil to her head and does not eat. The old priest has taught her this, to put oil on her head on fast days so she will look fresh. She will not look as if she is fasting, which she is in the habit of doing twice a week. She decides she will observe her fast whoever may be coming to see her. The temple is a place of worship but it is also her home, where she sleeps and eats. Sometimes there are strangers around and she tolerates them, but she will not change her day.

When she is called to the temple's inner courtyard she gets up too quickly. For a moment her head spins and she cannot feel the bones in her legs. She lets her watery limbs carry her out and she stands where the priest tells her to stand, at the top of the steps facing a courtyard full of men, some of whom have travelled a great distance to see her. The old priest who has taught her how to speak, the old man she calls Abba, this kindly old man cannot look her in the eye. The light in the courtyard is too bright. She can barely see the faces of the men. She knows only that there are too many of them and the sun is hot on her face. The old priest tells her not to squint. In a louder voice he asks her to tell the crowd her name. Mary, she says, too quietly. A man who is standing at the back tells her to say it again – her name, he cannot hear. She sees a broad face and a bushy black beard.

'Mary,' she says, louder this time.

'Sorry, I can't hear you,' says the man with the bushy beard, laughing. 'Can you say it one more time?'

She repeats her name and hopes it will be over quickly, the selling of her, because that is what the priest is doing. He will sell her. Or, worse, he will give her away for nothing.

The old priest sends a boy to gather stalks from the almond tree outside the temple. She knows the tree. It was her first playmate. The boy returns with a bundle of stalks clasped in his arms and the priest wraps a blanket around it. He asks each of the men to take one. As they come up to choose they look at her, some with curiosity, some shyly. One or two of the men do not look at her at all. When they have gone back to their places the priest asks the men to hold up the stalks they have chosen. Only one among them holds a flowering branch, its delicate pink flowers gathered in a bunch at the end. It is one of the men who would not look at her. She notices very little about him, but that he is very old. The others congratulate this man who cannot look at her and does not know what to do with her now that he is her husband.

The colour of sunlight shifts and the water in her legs settles in her feet. She cannot touch the world and its glittering surfaces, where everything is an arrangement of feathers. The world is a feather that might blow away. She wants to say this to the men but her voice will not leave her throat. She must learn how to speak and stand without falling. She must learn how to breathe. She closes her eyes for a moment. When she wakes she is inside the temple and a piece of wet linen is on her head. They have called a healer, who tells the priests she will be all right. Her old abba still cannot meet her eyes.

She is twelve years old.

After the day of her betrothal she does not see her husband again for a long time. Meanwhile her time of impurity begins. She must move from her room in the temple to live with the women who serve the priests. Her life goes on as before. She gathers water at the well. She cooks and serves. She continues with her lessons and her prayers. But there is a change in her. Her body is no longer hers. Or it has become hers in a way she could not have imagined. A few months after her time of impurity begins, it ends. Her body stops its monthly payments of blood. She tells the priest:

'My time of impurity has ended.'

'No, it hasn't.'

'If my monthly impurity has ended, why can't I return to the temple?'

'You think too much,' he says. 'Do you want to think or do you want to be happy?'

'Why can't I do both? I am happy, I think.'

'Work more, think less. Your impurity has not ended.'

It is only when she returns with one of the women that the old priest believes her. He summons her future husband, whose lamentations are loud enough to be heard throughout the temple. No, he keeps saying, as if by saying the word he will change the true sequence and she will be who she was. But none of his denials stills the tumult in her belly and the sickness she eats, the dullness at daybreak and the dreams that descend at any time of day or night, hot oily dreams that pick her up and throw her into waves of fluorescence. Her face changes with the hours. It is serene at midnight and creased with terror at dawn. She cries out in her sleep those names no one has heard. The old priest speaks with her old betrothed and over many days and nights they come to an agreement. Her future husband comes to her and takes her hands in his.

'You have been touched,' he tells her.

'No,' she says. 'I have not.'

'Not by a man but by an angel,' the old man says.

'I have been touched by no one,' she says, looking at his brown hands on her own, 'except you.'

'My life is yours. I give myself to you and to the child you carry, as protector, as provider, as father and husband.'

Then begins her time of happiness, when she understands that the world is not feather but bird. It was created to be grasped. Its glitter is reflection, not simulation, and its people are subject to the same cares and joys as she. How can they not be? They too are mortal, subject to illness and pleasure, trying to build a home for those they love.

At the end of her life, at the foot of the cross on which her son is stretched, she is once again the girl who is given away. There is no more than a single breath between her son and the time of his dying, yet he finds the need to put forward a substitute. A new son who will not abandon his mother. Perhaps he sees the emptiness that will surround her. Does he think so little of her, that she will accept some other as son? For he tilts his head towards the one called John and he gives away his mother with three words: *Behold thy son.* How can she believe in the truth of words? This John is not her son and she is not his mother. She is not the mother of every stray boy or man who happens to fall into her line of sight. How can she believe in words when they cause such confusion? How can she believe in anything when all that has befallen has crushed her belief and demolished hope?

She does not know how long she stays there, keeping her eyes on her son's twisted form changing now in the light of the first stars. She is his mother and there is nothing about his body that she does not know, but here on the cross he appears to her as a stranger in need. Later a dull red moon appears. His slender body is indistinguishable from the shadows on the hill. She is ashamed to experience the darkness as a blessing. Around them torches are lit. From time to time she hears a ragged breath or a broken word or the cries of men in agony. She does not know if it is her son or the others who are some distance from him. Two young men who are also suffering, whose mothers and wives are far away. She cannot hear them clearly and this too is a blessing. Towards morning, folded into herself amidst the group of women who have stayed with her son, she closes her eyes to a bedlam of images. To remember is to see a world so terribly changed that she is grateful she will soon be gone from it. Fear has come and it will never leave. This much is clear from the faces she sees around her, each with its own share of bewilderment or grief.

As a child of the temple her life had a certain order imposed by its surroundings. She went to the well each morning. She said her prayers. Meals were served and eaten in the same room at the same time. Her life was ordered and her mind was chaos. From the window she saw the packed earth of the road in all weathers and the people who came to the temple, the fathers and mothers and children. The parents did not give their children away. The little ones staggered upon the earth as if it was theirs. A foundation on which they could depend. Most of her hours were spent alone. She searched the sky for a sign that she belonged to someone and someone belonged to her and there was a design in the things she saw and touched. She tried to believe in the solidity of things. This was her cruellest burden, that she was required to believe and could not.

The world had cracked and would fly apart at any moment.

One day the priest sent her to the market to buy a honeycomb. In a noisy grove set apart from the main square she found a man covered from head to toe in muslin. She stood as close as she could to the dark hives and wished the creatures would descend on her and cover her with life and mark her with their barbed wilful kisses. They anticipated each other and danced towards one another. The hive was one vast creature bursting with life. She lost all sense of herself as she watched one of the bees. He was constantly on guard. He had two hairy eyes and around his two eyes were many smaller ones and this was how he kept account. It was how the bees stayed together and loved each other and sang in harmony. It seemed as if they were slaves, but they were builders. There were thousands of them, each in service to their ancient and exacting order. She stood there for a long time and forgot why she had come. The sound beat against her ears. She watched the bees and longed for the mother she had hardly known. She listened to the bees at their work and longed for great work of her own. At last the world became real to her and she knew its workings. Only a unifying intelligence could have created it.

At the foot of the cross she looks up at her son in the indifferent light and she remembers the bees as her first experience of joy. The memory leads to another. On the day after the Sabbath, not long after her son is born, murder arrives at their doorstep in the shape of the King's new law. Her husband tells her to prepare for a long journey to a country she has never before visited. They leave everything except what they can carry and take the road that winds by the sea, a road so long she is sure it will never end. For weeks they follow the coast and travel in the day and rest at night wherever they can, the infant always in her

arms. It is at this time of upheaval that she learns to love
her husband. His years seem to melt away in the daily
rigour of the journey. She sees he has been made youthful
by their flight.

Even then, when her son was an infant, they knew that
keeping him safe was the most important thing either of
them would do in their lives. Early on the second day they
stopped near a grove of fig trees and ate some of the food
they had packed. She heard the sound of water and went
to find it while her husband threw his elbow over his eyes
to rest. It was her second memory of happiness. With the
sun in her eyes and her son in her arms and her husband
nearby, she followed the sound of fresh water. The bank
was noisy and filled with life, a hundred unhurried insects
tangled in the undergrowth. She dipped into sleep for a
few minutes and woke without cares or worries, a young
woman on a task of great importance. Mother and son
woke together and she felt his whole life in her arms.

How soon the laughter turned to tears. How often the
one followed the other. Until she learned to mistrust all
but the laughter of infants. She learned to suppress laughter,
for the road was long and full of enemies. She learned to
hide her joy and her son learned this too. Like her, he
preferred the comfort of melancholy. But when did he lose
his regard for his mother? When did he stop thinking of
her as the bearer of his world and the repository of his
secrets? Did he not know that she would never abandon
him or give him up? When was it that he stopped loving
only his mother and expanded his love, letting it grow and
grow until it encompassed the whole world? If there was

a moment when it happened, she wanted now to return to it and change it.

He was so young. A boy who took to the new country in a way she and her husband could not. He understood the breathing singsong tongue and the soft hard phrases that he learned to say so quickly. He understood their thinking in a way he did not understand his parents. He liked them, that was the truth of it. He liked the language and the mystifying habits. The incomprehensible names. The bewildering array of gods, thousands upon thousands who ruled every aspect of their world. Gods in the shape of dogs and snakes and monkeys. Gods who took the form of the sun and the wind. Gods in the guise of the dead, returned to watch over the living. Gods as kings and queens and demons. Gods of language and knowledge. Gods who appeared as a tree or a river, or a tree in the river. So many gods it was impossible to keep count of them all, until it seemed to her that everything was a god in the new country. And it was her son who told her these things, that those who worshipped the thousand gods had discovered the true shape of the world. Within the many they were worshipping just the one.

It was when they returned from the other country that the terrible changes began. He lost all interest in his mother. He went for days without a word or a glance in her direction. If she approached him with a smile or a platter of food, he turned away from her as if she had done something wrong. He left home the same way, without a word or a glance. She did not know where he had gone. It was Lydia who told her that he was going to the river to see the Baptist, a journey of some days. He returned a different man, changed entirely, sufficient unto himself. He had no need of his mother. He was unable to meet her eye but deigned to smile in her general direction. The smile of a king bestowing favour upon a subject. He remembered nothing of his early life and wished never to speak of it. It was clear that he had forgotten his old dead father who spent the last years of his life protecting them. He was in a haste to forget his mother. Then he disappeared for good. He would go to the mountains to think, he told her, as if he could not think at home in the presence of his mother. She did not know then that it was one of the last times she would see him alive.

She knows she is alone now. A woman who has lost her husband and her son to the new world, where the city has become a place of war in which soldiers rehearse their killings and priests sell themselves to whoever is the ruler. The sky changes colour from one day to the next. The smell of cooking or burning arrives on the wind.

Much later she heard he had returned and she went to see him. His brothers and sisters went with her. The crowd was frightening and some of the men were intent only on trouble. Unable to get near him they sent word that his mother and his brothers and sisters were waiting outside. The crowd surged and thinned and they kept waiting and then came news. He told those who were gathered: *I have no family but you. Who is my mother and who are my brothers? Here are my mother and my brothers.* He did not even mention his sisters, who loved him. It seemed to her then that his few words had called her life into question. *Who is my mother?* He had denied her. She was not his mother and he was not her son. He had said so. She was not his mother because his mother was elsewhere. With those few words he had taken away the thing in her life that had been hers and no one else's. He had taken himself away and left her nothing.

Now on the hill at the end of her son's life and not long before the end of her own, she remembers the night she gave birth. Dusty from travel, she and her sweet husband were ready to stop for the night. But there was nothing, not an inn, not a house. They thought they would rest until dawn and then look for a dwelling of some kind. Tired, her belly swollen, she sat on the side of the road and looked up at the night sky. Dry stems of grass pressed into the rough fabric of her tunic and into her flesh, but she could not get up. There was a sudden tug inside her and she cried out. Her time was upon her. She clutched at handfuls of grass and mud. Her husband found a rough shed hidden from the road and carried her there. The hot smell of animals fell upon her and made her want to vomit. On the floor, on a pile of new hay, she brought her son into the world.

It was the time of happiness. So many stars in the sky that anything seemed possible, dawn just hours away, the morning's new sunshine and the new life that would live for them all. She remembers that night and the days and nights that followed. She was happy then because she did not know that it would be taken away. Soon all would be gone, the hope of life and the chance for happiness. All would turn to ashes in the world to come.

Mary, wife of Joseph and mother of Jesus.

# 24

Mary, write that when I came out of the dream I was no longer a child of seven or a man of twenty. I was one man and all men and I was splintered on a beam of wood. I was the carpenter broken by his own tools. My posture of supplication, seeking succour, knees bent and useless, no longer conscious of the body I have come to loathe, object for men to taunt with spears, foot placed over foot, wrists tied and nailed, ribs cracked, learning the sound of my body leaving me and awake only in my head. Write that there is no sin but ignorance. To know is to know the knowable god, for the greater God is unknowable. To know the god is to know the lesser god who made the world in six days, made *day* and *night*, made light and dark and the divisions in between, made as many hours as there are joints in the fingers, made the free wobble of the earth and the fixed wobble of the stars, worked six days on the heaven and the earth and divided the waters with a firmament, water above and water below and dry land in between, and upon the land the timekeeper trees, whose sharp invisible threads are hair birds that feed on the wells of the flowers, made all of this. I ask my knowable father, shall I hymn thee? I ask my unknowable father, how shall I hymn thee? In time he replies. To perfect the baptism of water is to empty it of death. Thus do I go down into the water and thus do I not go into death, in order that I may be poured into the world. The Baptist it was who washed me to bring me to myself. He said to me I would die upon the cross and so I knew him as the true John. The heaven did not open. No voice said, you are my son and I am well pleased. No sign stood upon the earth or the sky. Before I left him in Jordan I scolded the Baptist, for I had heard of his words to those who came to be baptised. How he spurned them and called them vipers. I said to him then as I say to you now, exalt the lowest and the lowly in heart. For I too am lowly. All things come alike to all. Tend to the sunrises you are vouchsafed and the knowledge you are vouchsafed. When they say to you that I died for your sins, do not believe them. My God does not require blood sacrifice. My God is myself and you, my mother and my sister, Mary.

penguin.co.uk/vintage